This was completely different from the kisses I'd shared with Jinhyeok, the kiss I'd had with Dalmi. I realized I had wanted this feeling, I realized I had been missing this deep down in my bones, even though I had never experienced it before. The fact that I wasn't allowed to enjoy it made me focus on how much I enjoyed it.

THE
CRUSTACEAN

THE CRUSTACEAN

By Jang Jinyeong

Translated from the Korean by Chi-Young Kim

brazen

First edition

CHICHISAEGA SANEUN SUP
By Jang Jinyeong
Copyright © Jang Jinyeong, 2023, 2025
All rights reserved
Original Korean edition published by Minumsa Publishing Co., Ltd., in 2023.
English translation rights reserved by OCTOPUS PUBLISHING GROUP
LIMITED, under the license granted by Minumsa Publishing Co., Ltd.
Through Casanovas & Lynch Literary Agency, Spain.

First published in Great Britain in 2025 by Brazen, an imprint of
Octopus Publishing Group Ltd
Carmelite House
50 Victoria Embankment
London EC4Y 0DZ
www.octopusbooks.co.uk

An Hachette UK Company
www.hachette.co.uk

The authorized representative in the EEA is Hachette Ireland,
8 Castlecourt Centre, Dublin 15, D15 XTP3, Ireland (email: info@hbgi.ie)

Text copyright © Jang Jinyeong, 2023, 2025
Translation copyright © Chi-Young Kim, 2025

ISBN (hardback): 978-1-84091-910-3
ISBN (trade paperback): 978-1-84091-914-1
ISBN (ebook): 978-1-84091-912-7

A CIP catalogue record for this book is available from the British Library.

Typeset in 10.5/16pt Swift LT Std by Six Red Marbles UK, Thetford, Norfolk.

Printed and bound in Great Britain

1 3 5 7 9 10 8 6 4 2

This FSC® label means that materials used for the product have been
responsibly sourced.

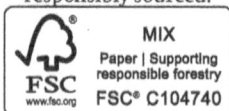

MIX
Paper | Supporting
responsible forestry
FSC
www.fsc.org   FSC® C104740

1

My name is Chichirim. Which means the woods where the chichibird lives. A chichibird is an incredibly rare, priceless creature; nobody is certain that it really exists. Only someone with a pure heart can see this bird. A chichibird is a harbinger of good luck.

I was called Hongikingan when I was young. Which means humanitarian. Not because my surname is Hong, not because I am a benefit to the world, but because my face was always flushed. *Hong*: red. *Ik*: ripe. *Ingan*: person. A ripe-red person. I like to delude myself that my red face was the reason I was an outcast in elementary school. That spring, when I was twelve, I wasn't Chichirim yet. But she was who I would become in the span of a month.

That was the year I was assigned to the absolute worst junior high, thanks to the lottery system that people referred to as the 'wheel of fortune'. To phrase it more elegantly, they were aiming for standardization. We still sat for placement tests, though, to ensure that each classroom was more or less homogenous, in an attempt to avoid all different levels being mashed together. That era was obsessed with standardization. I remember the general mood of the time as one that vilified the act of dividing and lining up and comparing. Which meant, ironically, that we longed for it. Everyone studied hard for the placement test; some of us listened to our sixth-grade teacher's plea to do well while others felt pressured to make a good first impression in junior high. None of it mattered, though. Because the lottery was what determined everything.

Onjo Junior High was seven or eight stops away on the bus. Onjo had been my third and last choice not just because it was far away but also because of its awful uniforms, the colours morose and ominous. Those uniforms played a big part in our hatred for Onjo. Actually that was the sole reason all of us hated it. Their winter uniform was the dull hue of red-bean porridge and their summer uniform was the pallid colour of green peas. Colours that were hard to define, colours that were depressing and made you feel a tickle in your nose, which made you laugh. The uniform was unfortunate but it was someone else's misfortune. Until, of course, I was assigned there. Just a few months earlier I was laughing at Onjo students, saying they looked like criminals locked up in prison. Because I sure wasn't going there. It never occurred to me that it would end up being my school. I was no criminal! I never spat gum on the sidewalk. I never jaywalked. So why was this happening to me?

Almost everyone else was assigned to their first or second choices. I was one of the only ones thrown into the school I never wanted to go to. It was my third and last choice, which I'd written down only as a formality so as to fill the box. Was it because my grades were worse than theirs? Hell no. Although it had only been a brief moment of glory, I had ranked number two in my entire grade. Was it because I didn't cheer for South Korea during the World Cup? Was it that I didn't rush out to buy a Red Devils t-shirt? Even though I didn't buy one, they won. I still didn't buy one and they still won. I gritted my teeth and held firm but then they won yet again. In the end, I gave in to the collective madness. I let an art student paint a soccer ball on my cheek and bought a red t-shirt from the back of a pickup. I joined the masses, I became a drop of water swept along with the tide. I felt safe but ashamed. I felt weird and helpless. The paint dried and shrivelled on my cheekbone, pulling my skin tight. By the time the game started, the soccer ball on my face had cracked open like an ancient fresco and had begun to flake. The words *Be the Reds!* printed on my belatedly purchased t-shirt were bound to meet a similar fate after a few washes. Though, as it turned out, I would only wear it that one time. They lost to Germany that day.

When Onjo students sang their school song, they changed 'Junior High' to 'Prison', the way they had done in each of their elementary schools. I'm sure kids are changing the lyrics in all the schools, even now. This happens organically, even if the idea isn't discussed among the kids first. This phenomenon always amazed me. Maybe that urge was stored in our DNA, like how the word for 'Mum' in most languages contains the 'm' sound.

'Such and such mountain, such and such river, clear spirit, strong and brave and resolute and courageous, blah blah blah, Onjo Prison.'

Whenever I sang the revised lyrics, I felt a stab of guilt — because I was now wearing a prison uniform. Not in the way some people talked about school. For the crime of being a student, they'd say, you're locked up in school, in a classroom, your name on the roll, wearing a uniform, and your punishment is to study until graduation. But Onjo Junior High wasn't metaphorically a prison. It was a brutal fact. Why did I have to go to Onjo? Why?

'Why is this happening to me?' I asked the doctor.

'Not everything has a root cause,' the doctor replied.

That sounded somewhat romantic. Not something a dermatologist should say. If she were a psychiatrist, maybe. It wouldn't be out of the ordinary to hear something like this while lying on a soft couch, sipping chamomile tea. The fabric covering the sofa would have some kind of special coating on it that made it easy to wipe away spillages. Because the patient would always be drinking tea lying down. Anyway, I digress; her answer wasn't right. A dermatologist shouldn't say something like that. Dermatologists are fundamentally car mechanics. They have to know what causes a problem. Imagine going to a garage because something's wrong with your car and the mechanic says that to you – *Not everything has a root cause*? The only way to reply to him would be to say, *What the fuck.*

As a teen my only skin problems were a few zits on my chin, but once I became an adult – in fact, years into adulthood – I had developed sensitive, itchy skin. Perhaps it was because I'd binned my shampoo and body wash and begun using an all-in-one product in an attempt at minimalism. The very same kind that men who can't be bothered to tote around various specialized products used at the gym. The bottle was blue and had a typical 'cool water' scent. The onset of my skin problems coincided with when I began to use this product. The itchiness started at my scalp and quickly spread all over my body. I was unbearably itchy; when I looked in the mirror, I looked dirty.

It had to be that all-in-one product. I was confident with my deduction. But, even when I stopped using it, I was still itchy. I began frequenting doctors' offices, moving to increasingly larger practices where it became increasingly more difficult to get an appointment, and I submitted myself for every possible test. One practice said that a test I'd done at another practice was pointless. 'Why is this happening to me?' I asked at the last doctor's office I visited – I think it was at Boramae Medical Centre – and that dermatologist was the one who told me that not everything has a root cause.

I called my sister to tell her this, and she was infuriated. 'But isn't it her job to figure out what the cause is?'

'Eonni,' I said, my tone surprising me; it was much warmer than I'd intended, perhaps I had been moved by her fury on my behalf. 'If you could be reborn, what would you want to be?'

'I don't want to be reborn.'

I had nothing to say to the fact she didn't want to be reborn. Honestly I wasn't even interested. I just wanted her to ask me the question back. So I stayed quiet.

'What about you?' she asked begrudgingly.

'I want to come back as a crab.'

'As crap?'

'Crab.' I put my forefinger and middle finger together like a claw and clacked them together. But then I remembered we weren't on a video call and quickly shoved my claw between my thighs. 'The crustacean.'

My sister let out a long sigh which lasted ten seconds. She was clearly thinking, *Grow up already, why don't you.*

'Why?'

'A crab's skin is made of bone and its flesh is under the bone. But we're the opposite. We have bone under flesh.'

I scratched myself, my skin festering like an overripe persimmon. That doctor had also said: 'Don't scratch yourself mindlessly. You can scratch if it's unbearable. I understand that's not something you can force yourself to stop doing altogether, but at least be aware that you're scratching.' What difference would it make if I recognized that I was scratching myself? It wasn't like my skin would be any less irritated if I scratched myself while being cognizant that I was scratching myself. She was ridiculously wrong. I didn't like her. I wasn't satisfied.

'I want skin made of steel.'

'Want to know how you can become a crab?' She suddenly sounded like she was right next to me. I almost looked around to see if she had walked over. 'You don't have to wait until your next life.'

Was she telling me I should die?

'How?' I asked.

'Scratch yourself. Just keep scratching away. Scratch everything all over. Then you'll scab all over,' my sister said coolly, 'like a crab.'

'That's cute.'

My sister snort-laughed, then cleared her throat, embarrassed.

The magical phrase *that's cute* always made us laugh regardless of what we were talking about. It was even funnier if it had nothing to do with the topic at hand. Long ago we had laughed over an internet meme, and afterwards we'd started adding *that's cute* after everything.

'I'm going to the bathroom.' 'That's cute.'

'My pants are too small.' 'That's cute.'

'I got dumped.' 'That's cute.'

'Have some broth, too.' 'That's cute.'

'What time is it?' 'That's cute.'

'Grandma passed away.' 'That's cute.'

'Why did you do that to me back then?' 'That's cute.'

The effect of *that's cute* was cute.

In other words, *wrong*.

Since we didn't have much in common or share many childhood memories, stupid jokes like *that's cute* were useful, even priceless. See, my sister was much older than me. So much so that when we were young, the neighbourhood women would wink at our parents and joke, 'You must have great chemistry.' Here, 'chemistry' meant *sex life*. Dad hinted at his virility by moving his body in a suggestive way while Mum pretended to try to get him to stop, feigning embarrassment while still being boastful. The reason I know all this is because my parents weren't careful about what I saw or heard them say. They thought I was a random lump of flesh that was entirely ignorant of sex. Or they just didn't care. They *clearly* didn't care. Our house was always overrun with women because Mum worked from home, tattooing eyebrows.

And, somewhat ridiculously, Dad was also always home, too. Dad sometimes went out for this or that job, but he never really revealed exactly what he did. When he got work, he did it, and when he didn't, he didn't. He never went looking for work. Dad and work were forced into an unrequited relationship; work had a crush on Dad but Dad loved Mum more than work.

He brought numbing cream over to Mum when her hands were encased in gloves, he served clients barley tea and he helped out with whatever else was needed during a tattoo session. He was basically a gofer. Mum's clients were equally jealous that she was treated like a princess and scornful of Dad, who was a bum. They were both envious and contemptuous.

My sister got herself hired as a bookkeeper at a Samsung Electronics Field Office the moment she graduated from her girls' vocational high school, and she lived in the company dorms and only came home out of duty or when she had to visit my school for administrative matters; otherwise she never dealt with Mum's clients. My sister hated these women, hated their behaviour and their small talk. In fact, she despised their conversations about chemistry and love and all that stuff. Hearing them chatter made her feel like she was the byproduct of our parents' horrific, disgusting love, as though she were evidence left behind by an inattentive criminal right at the crime scene. 'Those *people* have nothing to do with me,' she would say; our parents were 'those people'. She harboured a lot of resentment, which I didn't fully understand yet because I hadn't lived with our parents for as long as she had. I was only twelve, though I would turn thirteen in a month.

The lockers at Onjo Junior High were in the hallway, not in the classrooms. They weren't the cool, tall ones you saw in American teen movies, so, between classes I would sit cross-legged on top of them. By now, I had developed my own dirty, disgusting, thrilling secret hobby of making sure people could see my polka-dot underwear under my skirt. I'd begun to pick out the brightest underwear on purpose so everyone walking by could see them. You see, I didn't wear stockings or undershorts, just socks on bare legs. I'd shaved my legs the day before but the hair had grown out a bit. It was early in the semester, early spring, when it might still snow but the weather wasn't too cold, so I could. During the breaks boys hovered by the lockers, pretending to look for their textbooks or recorders or gym uniforms. The boys had started growing taller than girls at this time. Before, they had been around our height or smaller, but now they were shooting up in a growth spurt which started later than for us girls. But from my perch on top of the lockers I could still look haughtily down on them. At their shorn necks and their pale scalps visible through their hair. I could feel the vibrations of the locker doors opening and closing on my butt and thighs. The lockers' cool metal surface beneath me had been warmed by my tepid skin. And then, just as I felt someone's gaze, I would innocently drop my legs and swing them in the air, before sitting cross-legged again, making sure they saw my polka-dot underwear.

'Hey, I can see the wings on your pad,' Dalmi whispered to me, her thumbs hooked in the pockets of her red-bean-porridge jacket. My eyes caressed the fabric of her jacket. I engraved its texture into my pupils. She'd clearly bought her uniform from the official store as her jacket wasn't made out of the shiny non-woven fabric that mine was. Everyone at school could tell instantly where you had bought your uniform from, though to the uninitiated they all looked like the same gloomy red-bean porridge. But now that I was at Onjo, I obsessed over the minute differences in material and colour and texture of uniforms from different vendors. A beaded phone charm dangled out of the pocket of Dalmi's jacket. The beads looked like gummy bears. I wondered whether they looked more like bears or gummies. After all, which was closer, when something was copied from something that was itself a copy? If I asked my sister nowadays, twenty years later, she would tell me to shut up. *Why is that important? Get your head on straight. Be sensible. Speak coherently. What the hell are you trying to say? You're driving me insane.* And then, without getting my feelings hurt, I would strike back with, *That's cute.* I would make her laugh. Even though I wanted to ask, *Why did you do that to me back then?*

But back then, we hadn't started peppering *that's cute* in our conversations. Back then, we were both incredibly earnest and serious. That was why I couldn't ask her if they'd looked more like bears or like gummies. And I also couldn't ask her because she lived in the dorms, out in the boonies. The day she packed up her things, I asked, 'Isn't Samsung Electronics a huge company? Then why are you all the way out there? Why aren't you in Seoul?' She glared at me before she left, slamming the steel front door behind her. The sheer force of her slam made a dent in the door.

Anyway, the beads on Dalmi's phone charm were translucent light-yellow plastic, which morphed into various different colours depending on the light. I had the same charm on my phone, in my pocket. Beads that looked like bears or like gummies. We had bought them as a matching set at the stationery store. Of course we weren't *going out.* Back then, it was just cool to buy matching sets, no matter what they were.

Among our elementary school peers, Dalmi was known as the girl who was stupid unlucky. Alongside me. Because we were assigned to Onjo Junior High.

I wasn't that close to Dalmi in elementary school. I knew who she was but that was about it. We had different friend groups and we didn't even say hi when we bumped into each other. I don't know what Dalmi would have said about me. We only ended up hanging out in junior high because we were assigned to the same classroom, because we had gone to the same elementary school and because we had the same stupid bad luck. I was super relieved that we had become friends, since making a best friend and not being a loner was the most important thing at the beginning of every year. So, I was relieved, but at the same time afraid that I would be left behind somehow, or betrayed. You see, in fourth or fifth grade, Dalmi had manipulated the other girls to turn me into an outcast, but by the time we got to junior high, it was as though she had completely forgotten about her behaviour back then. As though none of it was her fault, not the isolating-me part nor the forgetting part. I guess everyone gets ostracized at least once in their lives for being weird, for being different? Everyone gets bullied, then turns around and bullies someone else, and then gets bullied again, and then, in order not to get ostracized again, bullies someone else. This happens *all* the time. Though it was Dalmi who was always freezing someone out.

When he heard the word *pad*, the boy who had been glancing over in my direction, ostensibly for his gym kit even though he didn't have PE next period, flinched and slammed his locker shut. The tips of his ears turned red. I feigned complete surprise and lowered my legs and made sure my lips didn't curve into a smile. I had forgotten that I was on my period. It would have been better if I'd remembered. Better for me, not for the peeping boys.

I first got my period at Makttungi Uncle's restaurant. He was my mum's little brother. That was over a year ago, when I was still in sixth grade. We were at the soft opening of the restaurant and free food was being served. Octopus soup and octopus bibimbap. The restaurant was stuffed to the gills with our family celebrating the opening and others who'd come for the free octopus. Sadly, that turned out to be the busiest day the restaurant ever had. Later, Makttungi Uncle's restaurant would shutter. Despite meagre sales it would manage to stay open for almost twenty years, hardly ever making a profit, but eventually it collapsed in the aftermath of the pandemic. Makttungi Uncle didn't know this yet, though; at his soft launch he was full of false, rose-tinted hope. Congratulatory flower arrangements and plants were delivered because no one knew then that, twenty years later, the restaurant's fate was to wither and die. That night, the flowers kept coming until the restaurant resembled a botanical garden. Makttungi Aunt organized the flowers and ordered the employees around. People rang the bell at their tables every ten seconds.

'Mum, I'm bleeding,' I whispered, pulling her sleeve. 'My stomach hurts. No, no, it's not that. It's not.'

Mum acted like an annoyed cow flicking her tail to shoo a fly away. Eventually she realized that it was my period, and yelled out, 'Anyone have a pad?' in exactly the same way a server would call out, 'Who ordered the jjajangmyeon?' A woman pulled a pad out of her purse and handed it to the person next to her, and it moved from hand to hand like a love letter until it finally reached me. Everyone clapped maniacally then. It was the first time in my life that I was congratulated by so many people. And the last. Makttungi Uncle was probably disappointed that all the attention had turned away from him and his soft launch. Telling you this makes me want to apologize to Makttungi Uncle even now. Uncle, I'm sorry. I'm sorry I got my period on the day you opened your restaurant, of all days. (I called him Makttungi Uncle before I realized that *Makttungi* meant *the baby*. I thought Makttungi was his name.) He was fat and balding. I thought his name was Makttungi because he was ttungttung – fat. I'm sorry, Uncle. I'm sorry I thought your name was Fatty.

Right now, I want to grab everyone and apologize because I want an apology myself. I'm sure my sister would get mad at me if I told her this.

So, where was I? Yes, as everyone applauded my entry into womanhood, Mum sent me to the bathroom. I clung on to the pad, terrified. 'How did it work?' I asked her, but she just said it was obvious when you opened it up. Which was true. I understood the instant I opened the pad. You see, Mum wasn't the attentive type. I didn't even wear a bra when I'd grown boobs. I couldn't bring myself to ask her to buy me one because Dad was always by her side. And my tongue would incinerate and crumble if I had to utter the word 'bra' in front of Dad. Dad was a lovebug, a devoted husband, a servant. He loved her to death. To borrow my sister's words, he was a 'stupid loser'. If it hadn't been for my sister, I would have walked around for the rest of my life hunched over to prevent my nipples from showing through my top. The boys who would try to snap my bra strap would have been rendered speechless, their hands frozen in the air. Thank God my boobs started growing before my sister moved out to the boonies. Of course, they stopped growing when I started wearing an actual bra.

There was a tenuous connection between my hobby of sitting cross-legged on top of the lockers and my boobs mysteriously halting their development. See, I wasn't entirely convinced I was a girl. I felt like a lowly organism that hadn't fully evolved. So the least I could do was show my underwear. Especially since I was Dalmi's best friend and I knew our friendship was a temporary condition; I was a temporary best friend. A best friend only until she got a new best friend. This was an obvious truth that cut deep when I lay in bed every night.

Dalmi was tan and had a rack. In other words she was hot. In elementary school, she could get away with breaking the rules because she was hot. She was tall and had big boobs. That made her cool. At that age, physical attributes determined your social ranking. Being a good student meant nothing at all. Remember, it was an era besotted with standardization. An era in which you sat for tests but your grades remained a secret. Even if you were in the top two of your entire grade. Only after the entire student body put their heads together and compared and contrasted and crunched the numbers did I realize that I was the second best in our grade. I went home and boasted about it to Mum, who said, 'Can you bring me the numbing cream?' I bragged about it to Dad but he didn't hear me because he was giving Mum the numbing cream. My sister was counting down the days at her vocational high school so she could become a contributing member of society. So it was a client, lying on the bed with numbing cream and plastic wrap on her eyebrows, who said,

'Good for you!' Her eyebrows would soon swell red, irritated by the unsterilized needle, then fade into a mortifying blue. I don't remember if I was ostracized before I scored in the top two or after. Maybe it had nothing to do with grades. Maybe it was because I hung out with the losers. My best friend at the time was a girl named Sein. We played tag and jumped rope and drew pictures. The other kids treated us like we were mentally deficient. Or maybe it was just me they treated that way. Eventually Sein stabbed me in the back and began hanging out with Dalmi. She became Dalmi's puppet. She bullied me and made my life hell. But then Dalmi, the queen bee, was cast off to the same junior high as me. And we became best friends. Dalmi had a big rack. She was tan. Though pale skin was the standard of beauty, this didn't apply to Dalmi. Dalmi was Dalmi. I didn't sweat it. Even though I was someone who was forced to consider whether the silly rumour that drinking strawberry milk made your boobs grow was true or not. It was entirely fair that my boobs were small; it was divine providence. Obviously some kind of standardization had applied to our boobs. We were destined to be best friends.

Each grade at Onjo Junior High had a weird kid. Maybe it had to do with subsidies or a quota. Or maybe it was another attempt at standardization. The standardization of ability, the standardization of geography, the standardization of income level. Standard students. A stew of bits and bobs that boiled over. I don't know what the adults were dealing with, not then and not now. The way I still don't know how to calculate dates by the lunar calendar, even though I'm now over thirty. I get it when someone explains it to me, but I still can't figure it out the next time it comes up. Maybe I'll never figure it out. It's not that hard but I'm still perplexed by the lunar calendar. Who understands it?

Anyway, as I was saying, as a result of subsidies or a quota or standardization, we had a weird girl in my grade. We were the children of Boomers, and there were so many of us that the school had to build an annexe. There was a sickening number of kids. Only three of the seventh-grade classes were assigned to the annexe and the weird girl was in one of them. Dalmi and I weren't in her class, but we were in the annexe. The annexe, a jerry-built single-story structure, felt snug and remote, colder than the main building. The windows were so thin that the winds ripped through, howling, swaying the entire building. The movement made me sick to my stomach. And the weird girl would sometimes leave shit on the floor.

Something happened at every break. Everyone would rush over to see what she had done. Once I heard, *It's a snake!* I jumped off the lockers to take a look at her shit but it really was a snake. A young green snake slithering among dirty indoor shoes, bending its hundreds of joints. What if it got trampled? Maybe it had come down from the hill behind the annexe. The skinny thing flashed by like some kind of afterimage. It was the first time in my life that I saw a snake. And the last. The kids from the main building scoffed at us, saying we were bluffing. Even though we were arbitrarily assigned to the annexe, not based on grades or anything, there was a pervading sense that the main building kids looked down on us. Or maybe they were envious of us and tried to hide it. After all, the annexe was filled with adventure, and it had a cool, delinquent vibe. To be honest I can't be certain that I saw that green snake with my own two eyes. Maybe the murmurs of *It's a baby snake, did it come down from the hill* intermingled with dozens of feet stamping up clouds of dust in the hallway and got woven into a real memory. These days, whenever I meet someone new, I ask if they have ever seen a real live snake. To see if this 'snake' really exists in this world. No, I don't mean in books or on the screen, I tell them. In real life.

Sometimes the weird girl would pull up her blouse. I wasn't an enthusiastic participant but a few times I did get on my tiptoes and crane my neck, like a short person at a standing-room-only concert. She wore a white cotton bra. Her stomach was flat and her skin was flaky; maybe she was malnourished. She breathed rapidly. Her behaviour had no purpose, unlike mine; I had a clear purpose in mind when I sat cross-legged on top of the lockers. She was locked away in her own heightened, chaotic, noisy world.

'Ugh, this is boring.' Dalmi turned away haughtily from the crowd.

A terrible realization struck me like lightning. The boy who had been 'looking' for his gym uniform hadn't slammed his locker door when he heard Dalmi whisper, 'I can see the wings on your pad'; he had closed it before that, a few seconds earlier. When Dalmi came toward the lockers looking for her temporary best friend. Not because he was embarrassed to have been caught looking under my skirt but because he was more interested in Dalmi than in my polka-dot underwear, even with the wings of a pad stuck to them. This meant that I would never be able to compete with Dalmi, no matter how wide I opened my legs and even if I had angel wings stuck to me instead of the wings of a pad.

Right about now, you might be asking, 'So what are you trying to say here, what's this story about?'

The way my sister would, my sister who I want to kill. You might snap, 'Get to the point.'

Sorry, my story is getting long. Don't be mad. Not yet.

What I am trying to tell you is this: I wasn't pretty.

2

Everyone finds their own way to thrive. Being pretty is the best way, but if you aren't, then you can at least be a good student. And early on, I decided my path was to be a good student. I've already mentioned that I once landed in the top two of my entire grade and that damn drive for standardization made a mess of everything. Everyone had to be hush-hush about grades and rankings. Did someone kill themselves over their grades? How did we end up at such an abnormal, unnatural school? Even if you got good grades, nobody acknowledged it.

Like I mentioned before, I was ostracized in elementary school. I was treated like a nobody because I played tag in the yard instead of going to a noraebang or an arcade. Dalmi, who bought matching phone charms with me only because we were assigned to the same junior high, was starting to move toward new friends. She wanted a prettier friend. She hadn't realized that the advantage of being with me was that she could stand out. We were a great pair.

Still, I could see why Dalmi wanted a pretty girl by her. A rose is beautiful when it's surrounded by baby's breath. See, baby's breath is still a flower. And I was no flower. A rose's beauty is muted when it's surrounded by garbage; it would be overlooked. I was twelve and stupidly tried to ignore that fact. We managed to maintain our friendship for some time.

Because I was useful to her. It wasn't necessarily advantageous for her to be my friend but I was useful. She didn't have to cast around for a partner when she was in an odd-numbered group. She didn't have to go to the bathroom all alone or with a crowd. At lunch she could steal as many pieces of meat off my tray as she wanted. With me, Dalmi could do anything she wanted. I was relieved. Being useful was how I thrived during that time.

Dalmi also had several candidates for a boyfriend. She used me to get under their skin. This was how I ended up having my first-ever kiss with Dalmi. I always went over to Dalmi's after school. That was what she wanted me to do, so why would I refuse? She never told me, but from what I could gather, Dalmi was an only child and her parents were divorced. It was only her mum who was ever at home. Maybe it was a given that her dad wasn't there since most dads weren't home around four in the afternoon, but for some reason I got the feeling that her parents had split up. That made Dalmi seem even cooler. There weren't that many divorced families back then. It wouldn't have been cool for the weird girl at school to come from a broken family but Dalmi, as I said, was Dalmi.

Dalmi's mother was a taciturn woman. When we got there, she would start cooking without a word. I don't remember her mum ever saying anything to me. She didn't ask how school was or how my grades were. She didn't even ask me what my name was. I still remember the steamed egg she would make us. That's how good it was. It was a soft, damp steamed egg, different from the billowing kind with a scorched bottom that you got at barbecue joints or the sweet, pudding-like Japanese versions. I had never had steamed egg like hers before or since. She made it in a unique way, cooking it in the microwave instead of on the stove. Later, I tried to make it myself but it always turned out awful.

I quite want to see Dalmi's mum now and ask her, *How have you been?*

After school, Dalmi, her mum and I would sit at the table, eating in silence. Dalmi was a fast eater and would get up first. It was clear her parents had not taught her any manners. Getting up first when an adult was still eating? That kind of rude behaviour was one of the reasons I reckoned Dalmi's parents were divorced. Then again, it didn't seem like Dalmi's mum minded. Dalmi would place her dish in the sink then sit on the living room sofa and watch TV while her mum and I ate quietly across from each other. Sharing a meal with someone else's mum, someone who knew nothing about you and vice versa, was a very strange experience. Back then it felt weird but I sort of miss it now. It was a rare, peaceful moment for me. It felt as if I were being looked after with that damp steamed egg made in the microwave.

Not long ago, I drunk-dialled my ex after we had split and told him I wanted to eat his mum's marinated raw crab again. I'd never had marinated raw crab that good before or since. Her secret was to use only red pepper flakes in the marinade. That crab was in a different category altogether from all other marinated crab I had tried, which was always too sticky sweet. People who could cook have always impressed me.

When Dalmi's silent mum and I finished eating, she started the dishes and I went over to the sofa and flung myself next to Dalmi. The wooden frame of the sofa made a loud crack. I flinched but Dalmi didn't seem to care. She tended to remain indifferent to most things. (You see, she was naturally cool. A very rare attribute.) And we leaned against each other like a thatched-roof house made of two cards. We watched some silly programme that didn't require an ounce of concentration which made me feel both comfortable and relaxed. Dalmi took her phone out and showed me the texts from boys pining after her. Childish, pathetic messages. The beads shaped like bears, like gummies, dangled between her fingers. Their light-yellow plastic moulded to resemble crystal. In the sunlight they changed from one colour to another. Daylight radiated out around us like spilled orange juice as the sun set. Dishes clattered in the kitchen, the sound of everyday life. A ray of light refracted through the beads and settled on the clear indent between Dalmi's nose and mouth. Forming a rainbow.

'Let's take a picture,' Dalmi said, turning on her phone camera. The rainbow fled from view.

She switched to the front camera and our faces filled the screen. It was a flip phone so the screen was tiny – what was the model again, it was silver with a blue border – and her number started with 011. SK Telecom. My service was KTF so my number started with 016. (Naturally 011 numbers were cooler. Not necessarily just because Dalmi had one. Later, because 016 and 017 and 019 were so jealous, 011 would become extinct, along with all those other prefixes.) We craned our heads this way and that as we posed for the camera. I had to put extreme effort into looking pretty. I pulled my chin in and bugged my eyes open. Looks were different from grades. They were instant; they didn't require you to put in any work of comparing, contrasting, and putting together statistics. It was simple. Dalmi was pretty.

That was when I realized the truth – I would have to leave Dalmi's side. For her sake. Dalmi needed prettier people around her.

'Wanna give me a kiss?' asked Dalmi, still looking into the camera. Her eyes were staring right at me from the screen. I glanced toward the kitchen. I saw only the empty table. The sink was tucked around the corner. I could hear Dalmi's mum doing the dishes. *Wanna give me a kiss?* It was phrased as a request but it was really an order. I didn't dare disobey. I placed my lips against Dalmi's tanned cheek. The shutter clicked. I pulled my lips off her face and squinted at the screen. I looked like a dead fish caught three hours ago. Dalmi's eyes were lowered demurely. Dalmi was satisfied but I wasn't. We took a few more. Kissing Dalmi on the cheek again and again, I tried to convince myself that the pictures looked bad not because I was ugly but because of the unflattering angle. The dumb TV show ended and the commercials came on. Dalmi started to get bored so she came up with a solution that would put our appearance on more equal footing. She turned her head and placed her lips on mine. Click. The beads clattered against each other. Refracted light flew to the corner of the white wall. My eyes were closed in the picture and Dalmi's were open a crack, gazing at the bridge of my nose. Yes. That was it.

The sun eventually slumped behind a building, like an exhausted middle-aged man who collapses into a subway seat on his way home from work, and Dalmi's mum came out of the kitchen after finally finishing the dishes. I couldn't shake the impression that she had purposely taken a long time. Maybe I wasn't the first of Dalmi's friends to do this. It occurred to me that Dalmi's mum hadn't talked to her own daughter at the table, either. Weird. The TV turned black for a second, reflecting us tangled together on the couch. Dalmi texted the picture of us kissing to the pining boys.

I left Dalmi's building and slowly walked home. I picked up my pace and then ran as fast as I could. I was overwhelmed, miserable. Confused. I wanted to cry. My tears came not when I was sad but when I was confused. My heart hammered in my chest like a newly grown wing attempting flight. Like someone was trapped inside, punching me in the breastbone. A salty wetness hung in my mouth. The taste of the steamed egg. A taste created not by flames but by microwaves. A taste I had never experienced before and would never experience again.

I got home and walked through the front gate. I crossed the yard and tried to open the front door, still dented from that time my sister slammed it. It no longer fit in the frame properly so you had to put some force into it, lean back and yank as hard as you could. I remembered what Makttungi Aunt told me in their restaurant, that the men knocked when the bathroom door didn't open but women yanked. Apparently women tended to doubt their own strength instead of assuming the door was locked. I yanked the door as hard as I could. I tugged on it like I was the one trapped inside. There was no point in knocking or ringing the bell or using a key, because our house was never locked. None of us ever took a key anywhere because Mum ran her business out of the house. No business owner in the world would lock the doors during business hours. And since Dad was always home, too, we weren't afraid of burglars.

I heard something from the other side of the door. The click of the lock unlatching. It was now unlocked but they still didn't open the door for me. The dented front door remained closed, resolute as a wall. I flung it open, not at all worried. Inside, it was thick with smoke. Not from a fire or burning charcoal briquettes or anything like that. Tragically, tragedy never struck our family. Mum rushed into the bathroom as Dad opened every single window in the house, realizing that he couldn't follow her into the bathroom. Everything was hazy. I coughed. The smoke smelled delicious.

'Those people were eating grilled beef,' my sister told me as we sat in the Samsung Electronics cafeteria in the boonies. 'Have you ever had grilled beef?'

'No.' I spooned into my mouth the miyeok guk I had packed in a thermos.

I had made the soup for my sister's birthday, following tradition. I had left school early to arrive in time for her lunch break. I don't remember why I did such a mortifying thing. Did my first kiss make me lose my mind? When I texted to ask if she was coming home for her birthday, my sister responded, 'It's just another day, same as any other.' My sister liked to think of herself as sardonic. But really she was just uncool. I understood when I got there that it was a little too far to get to by public transit. You took a bus and got off at a random stop, then waited for an eternity only to take another bus before walking forever to get there. By the time I reached the front gates, I was panting, covered in sweat and dust.

'You're really not going to have any?' I offered for the thousandth time. The soup container was on the verge of overflowing with seaweed. I had brought even more soup in the rice container. I didn't want to go back home. Mum would keel over when she discovered that I had filled every pot we owned with seaweed. I had made it while Mum was poking a needle in an innocent client's eyebrows. A good cook would have soaked a teaspoon of dried seaweed in water to make one serving of miyeok guk. A teaspoon of seaweed! What an eye-opener.

'You eat it,' my sister said. 'I don't like miyeok guk.'

'But you do!' I felt betrayed. My voice sounded pitiful, which made me mad. 'You used to.'

'Do you like it?'

Now *that* was a hard question. How many Koreans were ever asked, 'Do you like miyeok guk?' It wasn't the kind of thing that ever occurred to you to ask yourself.

'I don't know.'

'That's because you've been brainwashed.' My sister banged her spoon on her metal tray as emphasis. She had decided to eat the company-provided lunch instead of the burdensome miyeok guk her little sister had personally cooked and ferried over. The other employees looked over at us. 'You've been brainwashed. To like seaweed.'

What the hell was she talking about? What parent brainwashed their child to like seaweed? It would make more sense to brainwash them into studying. How would it benefit anyone to like seaweed? But then I remembered going to a clothing store run by one of Mum's clients when I was little. They sold children's clothes but Mum didn't buy me any. They just sat around and gossiped. Mum had a terrible habit of taking me along everywhere, probably for the same reason Dalmi kept me around, because I was useful. For Mum it would have been boring to go out on her own and my sister had already become rebellious. And at that time Dad somehow did have a job. So, I was the perfect companion on her outings. I was quiet, I didn't grumble or whine, I was a Maltese puppy, a good listener.

While the two women lost themselves in gossip, I sat on a stool and suffered in silence for a torturous length of time, just staring at the clothes on display. So many frilly, beribboned outfits. The lady addressed me from time to time so I wouldn't get too bored. At least she was considerate. I would respond to her with a polite smile. You see, if you were ugly you had to at least be a good girl. As a matter of courtesy most adults told kids that they were pretty, but nobody had ever said anything nice to me about my appearance. It was clear what I was. The lady said, 'Oh, she's so—' then stopped talking, embarrassed. She couldn't bring herself to say I was pretty, not in good conscience. Instead, she said, 'She's so patient.' A few outings later, once Mum realized that there were issues with how I looked, she stopped taking me along. She took Dad instead. Well, maybe that's my inferiority complex talking. It could simply be that Dad had gone back to not working around that time.

'Are you talking about that clothing store?' I asked my sister. 'I remember that lady telling me that eating seaweed makes you pretty.'

'That's what I mean. That woman made that lady say that.' In my sister's lexicon, *that woman* meant Mum.

'Why?'

'To make you eat seaweed.'

'But why?' I ducked my head and shoved my spoon into the other container. I was already stuffed. 'Because I'm not pretty?'

'What is *that*?'

All the employees in the cafeteria were looking out the window. Dishware stopped clinking. It was as if something had come over everyone. Their eyes filled with awe, like they were looking at an impressive natural phenomenon. A black car was driving slowly by. Only after the car drove farther away did everyone begin talking at once. Like someone had pressed *Play* on a video tape that had paused. It had to be someone important.

'Is that Lee Kun-hee?'

My sister sighed, irritated. 'Why would the chairman come here? To the sticks?'

'Then who is it?'

'That's the assistant director of the audit department, from headquarters,' she said, poking her banchan with her chopsticks. 'You know how when the school commissioner visits the school and everyone cleans up the day before and the teachers show up in suits and they write down learning goals on the blackboard? And how you decide who's going to participate in class? He's someone like that, someone you have to be on your best behaviour for.'

Her explanation didn't quite make sense. Nobody looked at the school commissioner with awe like this. The way everyone had looked at the car was the way I gazed at Dalmi. People started getting up, one by one, having finished their lunches. I heard the women whispering, *the assistant director did this, the assistant director did that, the assistant director, the assistant director said. . .*It was how you would talk about a celebrity or someone you truly admired. The person in the black car wasn't like a commissioner. He was more like a rock star.

'Everyone must really like him,' I observed.

'Whatever,' my sister said apathetically. Then she grinned. 'I heard he's gay.'

These days I grumblingly refer to guys who would never be interested in me as gay, the way the fox talks about grapes out of his reach in the Aesop's fable, but that wasn't the case back then. Back then, being gay was a much more serious charge. I lost my appetite. My soup container was nearly empty and the rice container was about half full. And my sister was going to refuse to eat any of it to the bitter end. I screwed the tops on. As the seaweed ballooned in my stomach I felt like I was going to hurl.

'And you're not ugly,' she said as she opened the rice container and took a sip. 'To be honest, you're not pretty, but you're not ugly, either.'

'Give me back my soup.'

She handed it back without complaint. 'Anyway, they didn't brainwash you to like seaweed so you'd get prettier.'

'Then why?'

'Because it's cheap and plentiful. They think it's a waste to feed you beef. And *that*,' said my sister as she stood up with her empty tray, 'is the kind of people they are.'

3

The picture of our smooch that Dalmi sent to her pining suitors brought about an unexpected result. A boy, Jinhyeok, began pining after me, too. What the hell? It was unbelievable. Unfathomable. Why? Was it because he couldn't kiss Dalmi so he wanted to kiss her indirectly? To use me as a human mug, to put his lips on something Dalmi had once put her mouth on? Jinhyeok and I walked in Geunrin Park, near my house. He had come to see me. It was freezing, and late. A group of older teens were drinking in the gazebo. A stray dog roamed around. For the first time in my life, someone was telling me he liked me. I could barely keep it together; I was so excited to yank Jinhyeok's chain. I wanted to toy with someone's feelings like Dalmi did with mine. I wanted to get revenge on the world. Any doubts of *Why does he like me?* vanished. Now that I wanted Jinhyeok to like me, there was no need for useless doubts.

When Jinhyeok started texting me, I'd peeked at Dalmi's phone to check whether he was among the guys she was texting. He was. But only on occasion. Jinhyeok texted with Dalmi and with me. Sure, that could happen. But he was texting *me* more often. Dalmi's attention had to be distributed evenly and I had way more time on my hands. Or maybe he just liked me more. My phone's data plan allowed me to send a hundred texts a month. I used most of it on Jinhyeok. I stopped texting my sister and reserved a portion for Dalmi but made sure to text her less than before. My life was all about managing my limited resources. I didn't have big feelings for Jinhyeok but I still saved his texts in my permanent mailbox.

We sat on a scarred bench in the park.

'Want me to kill that asshole?' Jinhyeok asked grimly. He wasn't really asking. It sounded as though he had already decided he would.

I rubbed my left cheek, which was still swollen. Earlier that day, I had nodded off in English class. My trip out to the boonies had depleted me. The teacher ordered me to go stand at the back of the classroom but I dozed off there, too. I was told to go outside and get some cold air. It wasn't actually a punishment; she just felt bad for me. She assumed I had stayed up late studying. I was known as a good student, maybe because of the placement test. The teachers knew what our grades were even if we didn't. That came in handy in these situations. Otherwise I might have to try to seduce a teacher.

I walked down the chilly hallway, dragging my fingertips along the lockers. Would the hallway count as inside or outside? It was more outside than the classroom but more inside than the true outdoors and it was really too cold to go out. The wind rattled the windows, sounding like a bow scraping the thickest string. In the hallways of this jerry-built annexe, the weird girl shat herself and snakes slithered down from the hills. That was when I bumped into the dean of students, who was slapping a pool cue against his thigh. 'What are you doing?' he asked. I answered truthfully: 'Just getting some air.' Which was the truth. My English teacher had told me to go get some cold air. Perhaps I should have gone all the way outside. 'Just getting some air?' the dean parroted. 'Yes,' I said and then suddenly I was on the floor. Did I fall?

Once, during field day in elementary school, I'd been knocked unconscious when a swing hit me on the back of the head, and when I had come to, I had felt exactly the same as this. Now, I saw faces plastered on the classroom windows. Dozens of huge eyes. The dean swung his cue threateningly and the kids scattered, scurrying back to their seats. Suddenly the dean looked uncomfortable. He bent down and checked my face. 'Why would I hit you?' he asked, and rubbed his cheek against the very one he had just slapped. What the hell? I didn't know what to do. This action of his was more shocking than the actual slap. He had a big head and his breath smelled like instant coffee. 'There's no reason I would hit you,' he said, then left. I stood there for a long time, staring at the vanishing point of the hallway.

'It's the first time I ever got hit,' I told Jinhyeok. My cheek was still warm. I was less upset than intrigued.

'Whoa,' Jinhyeok looked stunned. Like an earthling spotting a UFO. 'Your mum never hit you?'

'No.' Of course not.

'Your dad?'

'No.' Dad? No way.

'They must really love you,' Jinhyeok said. Funnily enough, he sounded jealous.

I remembered what my sister had told me. *They think it's a waste to feed you beef. That is the kind of people they are.*

'They don't hit me because they don't love me. So it doesn't even occur to them to hit me.'

'So the dean loves you and that's why he hit you?'

'No.' That made no sense. 'Yeah. No. I don't know.'

Jinhyeok stretched his hand toward my left cheek. I flinched and leaned back. Or maybe I leaned back first and then he stretched his hand out.

Not everything has a root cause. I hadn't yet heard that line from the dermatologist because I was still only twelve at this point. I would only hear those words in an exam room at Boramae Medical Centre twenty years later. But when the dermatologist said that line to me, I felt as though I had already heard it before. Is it possible to remember the future? I knew it was: a cause didn't create an effect but an effect reflected the cause. The future forms the past. An effect comes before the cause.

Jinhyeok looked hurt. He had just wanted to lay his cold hand on my cheek to cool it.

'Do you really like me?' I asked, tamping down my desire to be cruel. Conditional clauses popped into my head, like *If you kill the dean, if you cool my cheek, if you stop texting Dalmi*. My heart ached when I thought about Dalmi. Was it because I liked Jinhyeok, or because Jinhyeok liked Dalmi, or because I liked Dalmi? I wasn't sure who I should feel jealous of.

He nodded. 'I wanna go out with you.'

Hundreds of conditional clauses spun like a slot machine in my head before gradually coming to a halt. 'Then do ten flips.'

The older kids were in the gazebo, laughing and swearing. The stray dog barked scoldingly. A bird's shadow flew by. A shadow, even though it was late at night. A homeless man lay down on the bench next to ours, tucked under newspaper. Without a word, Jinhyeok got up. With the toe of his sneakers he moved rocks and pebbles aside. The dirt looked hard; the ground was still frozen solid.

Jinhyeok couldn't do flips. He could flip partially but not complete full rotations, so he landed on his back instead of on two feet, slamming the back of his head and his butt on the ground each time. With each flip he made a dull thud. Blood rushed to his face. Thud. Thud. The ground trembled. The dark, still-icy ground.

I didn't tell him to stop. I counted out loud with a straight face.

I kept my romance under wraps. I didn't want Dalmi to know I was betraying her with Jinhyeok. And I wanted to remain close to Dalmi, close enough to kiss her. I wanted more. Jinhyeok kept quiet about it, too, even though we didn't ever promise to keep it a secret. I couldn't tell what he was thinking, but I was more confused by my own feelings.

Since I sat near the front of the classroom, I wasn't able to spy on Dalmi to my heart's content. Whenever I looked back at her, she was on her phone under her desk. Was she texting Jinhyeok? The teacher warned me to stop turning around. But I couldn't keep an eye on Jinhyeok, either, as he was a main building kid. I decide to allot one of my hundred texts per month to Dalmi in desperation: *whatcha doin?* No answer. I allocated another. Jinhyeok didn't answer, either. I tore a corner off my textbook and wrote: *whatcha doin?* and handed it to the kid behind me, saying it was for Dalmi. The note was delivered quickly. Everyone pitched in this way. Everyone was the sender and the recipient and the mail carrier. The note came back to me. Under *whatcha doin?* was the simple answer *thinking about you.* What a meaningless phrase. It was the same as saying *nothing.* When you typed *whatcha doin* on BuddyBuddy, everyone always replied *thinking about you.* It was a nice way of saying you couldn't be bothered to answer. When the dean asked what I was doing, maybe I should have told him 'thinking about you' instead of 'just getting some air'.

I decided to stop sitting cross-legged on top of the lockers. I would hate to be known as a slut, and for Jinhyeok to hear about it in the main building. I was sure he would break up with me. As he should be the only one to see my underwear. If he wanted to see it, that is. Or maybe he already knew about my secret habit? Perhaps that was why he told me he liked me? Because I seemed easy? I should buy sexy underwear from that cute store YES. The polka dots were babyish. I was sick of them. The lady who owned the clothing store had given us that underwear as payment for her eyebrows. We had heaps of underwear piled up at home. Enough to fill an entire room. I could wear a new pair a day until the day I died and never run out. That lady's husband ran a Ssangbangwool factory which had gone bankrupt during the IMF financial crisis. She should have paid for her eyebrows in bras. Then I wouldn't have had to hunch over when I started getting boobs. Then I wouldn't have been an outcast.

But I would be able to afford cute underwear at YES if I posted a thousand flyers. Mum had found me that job once I entered junior high. She had done the same for my sister. 'Make your own pocket money. Do you think food is free?' As if she had ever given me pocket money. I had never once received pocket money. I couldn't even buy snacks at the corner store. I had to just stand there, watching my friends tuck in. If I needed something, Mum bought me only that one thing I needed. So I was thrilled to have a job. I had basically gained freedom. I didn't have to ask for things. Money was sweet. Addictive. Private property all the way! Mum's clients, who owned various stores, became my employers. I started at the top floor of an apartment building, pasting a flyer on every door as I made my way down, one flight at a time. I made ten won a flyer, so I could earn around four hundred won in a standard apartment building where the elevator in each bay opened to two units facing each other. That was a huge amount.

I knew I might have to go to a vocational high school like my sister; she hadn't been a bad student, either. Sure, she hadn't been at the top of her class, but she also didn't blow off school. She could have gone to an academic high school. Generally people thought it was a crime not to go to an academic high school, but Mum thought otherwise. Mum wanted her to enter the workforce as soon as possible. To bring home money. To contribute to the family budget. Mum didn't know what elementary school or junior high we went to. She had zero interest. But, when it came to high school, she involved herself. As for Dad – pfft. Let's not even go there. Mum had given up on us because she was exhausted and spent, having had to raise all her siblings from a young age. I had no idea about Dad. Anyway, I was destined to go to a vocational high school like my sister. To work as a bookkeeper in the boonies. So there was no point in studying. I calculated how many apartment buildings I would have to hit up to save enough for YES underwear. I scribbled my calculations in the empty space in my textbook. What if Jinhyeok tried something before I could afford to buy the underwear? Should I throw away some of the flyers? The ladies who employed me didn't check whether I conscientiously did paste the flyers to doors.

So, it wouldn't matter if I threw away several dozen in a stack of flyers. Although I had heard that some mean operators did check up on you, going to a random building, heading up to a random floor, and checking, or looking through the apartment complex's trash bins. Of course the ladies who hired me didn't do that. There was trust between us because we saw each other every day at the tattoo studio that was basically a community centre, aka my house. But I still didn't want to try anything. The way I didn't spit gum on the street. Being ethical formed the foundation of my pitiful self-respect. It was the only way to feel superior to everyone else. That was the life of an ugly girl. Dalmi would be forgiven if she threw away flyers. But I wouldn't be. I might be slapped across the face. If it had been Dalmi who walked down the hallway 'to get some air', would the dean have hit her? Obviously not. He hit me because I was *me*.

I got another warning from my English teacher for looking back at Dalmi. But she didn't sound too firm. She sounded like she might be trying to hide her guilt, like she was about to burst into tears. She was gripping her own arm, like she was trying to stem a hole in an embankment. Like it might flood if she let go. She treated me gingerly. She had called me out a few times already but still wasn't getting angry. I think it was because I had been slapped across the face the last time she sent me outside. That wasn't the product of cause and effect, though. Cause and effect weren't formed that way. They were two independent events. I had the arrogant urge to reassure my English teacher that it wasn't her fault.

At break I went up to Dalmi's seat by the window. Girls who worshipped her were hanging around, so I had to wait my turn. But surprisingly she chose me and tugged me toward her by the wrist. I was shocked. The other girls glared at me and scattered. I was elated but at the same time terrified. I was certain I would be on the outs with her if my romance with Jinhyeok was discovered.

Dalmi snapped her phone shut and looked up at me. 'So you're going out with Jinhyeok?'

Did her discovery of my secret romance play a part in my pantsing Oksu? We played dodgeball during PE in the auditorium. I made sure to be out early so I could stand outside the lines. I hated PE. Who would like it? I hated changing into the uniform and going all the way to the auditorium. I hated the inertia of it, being annoyed at first but then ending up doing your best once you got there. And to make it worse, dodgeball was actually fun. I hated it all. Girls who were scared of the ball, and also scared of being out, screamed as they shuffled haphazardly in a cluster, including Oksu. She was small and dirty, and everyone whispered that she lived in an orphanage. She was always too loud.

After PE, one of Dalmi's worshippers pulled Oksu to one end of the auditorium. She was trying to suck up to Dalmi. I knew that urge very well. I knew it better than anyone. Dalmi must have frowned when Oksu screamed during dodgeball. She would have blamed Oksu for distracting her, for getting hit. Not her own reflexes that weren't fast enough. That frown indicated: *She's the reason I'm out. You make the first move before I tell you to. You do it. I'll stand guard.* In a mere second, with only a slightly arched eyebrow, Dalmi could give an order like that. She was a goddess. Our beautiful, diabolical goddess. Her loyal worshipper pushed Oksu into a space cocooned by heavy purple velvet curtains. She tugged Oksu's clothes off as Oksu struggled, protesting. Half a dozen girls were there. Dalmi, the most important, was there, and I was, too. Otherwise how would I know what happened next? Look, I'm trying to be honest. But this isn't a letter of apology.

'Take it off!' Dalmi's worshipper cried needlessly. I felt sad for her, that pitiful thing. *I'm sorry, but Dalmi isn't interested in you. Don't do anything stupid.* I knew with every inch of my being that Dalmi was testing me. Pride made my chest ache. 'Take it off!' Dalmi's worshipper shouted again. 'You crazy bitch. You stupid, crazy bitch. So, you can be a crazy bitch but I can't? I said, take it off, you crazy bitch!'

Held captive, Oksu whimpered and stumbled, flailing inside her clothes. Dalmi's expression didn't change. She didn't look at me. Which meant she was looking at me, at me only. I placed a hand on the worshipper's shoulder. That stupid bitch froze in shock. I jerked my head for her to move aside and she obediently stepped away from Oksu. She was clearly relieved. She had wanted someone to stop her. I swiftly stripped Oksu of her clothes. Like a social worker who had come to give her a bath. Like I had done this hundreds of times. Like this was my profession. Was I a good bully? Even someone who is ethical, who doesn't jaywalk or spit gum in the streets or throw away flyers, could bully the outcast. It felt like the smallest, most tender part of my heart had died, never again to be revived. I wanted to yawn; I was so bored and sick of everything. Out of nowhere I remembered the compliment the clothing store lady gave me. 'She's so – so patient.' I remembered what I had wanted to tell my English teacher, too. *It's not your fault, miss.* Finally, I pulled down

Oksu's underwear. Her disgusting wiry bush came into view. Even an orphan grows a bush, I thought. Oksu was buck naked. Yup, I had skills. Pretty badass.

All of that was merely an adorable act of revenge by Dalmi. Dalmi got back at me by making me pants Oksu. The word *revenge* feels too grandiose, too sickening. It was more like, *How dare you not tell me.* Dalmi didn't care about Jinhyeok. She probably thought, *Go out with him or don't go out with him, whatever.* That was all. All along, Jinhyeok had texted Dalmi to find out what I thought about him. And Dalmi wasn't the kind of girl whose self-regard would be damaged by the fact that Jinhyeok wasn't into her. She didn't care at all. A pretty girl was always generous. Still, she got her revenge. Because I kept my romance with Jinhyeok from her. Even though I didn't tell her because it had started after our eggy kiss.

Dalmi started seeing an older guy who went to a technical high school. The guys at our school pining after her had to accept their complete defeat. For us, the idea of a technical high school was like what your belly button smelled of. Off-limits and icky but something that forced you to take another whiff. An odour you missed when you couldn't smell it still. We vowed never to end up at a technical high school, but because of that, we ended up looking up to him. It was a swamp, a trap you couldn't extricate yourself from. Like the way you would think only about elephants if someone said to you, *Don't think about elephants!*

I was offended that Dalmi didn't want Jinhyeok. He suddenly seemed even lamer and stupider. I kept comparing him to Dalmi's boyfriend. Jinhyeok was immature. He was less sketchy, less hot. Our romance faded. It ended before it could really bloom. Jinhyeok, who couldn't do flips. Jinhyeok, who didn't land on his feet, all cool, but fell on his back. Thud. Thud. Thud. Jinhyeok, who tried ten times and failed every single time. Stubborn Jinhyeok, who ended up doing all ten flips like he was undergoing punishment. Scrupulous Jinhyeok, who knew he couldn't do them and so pushed the rocks and pebbles aside before he attempted them. Did I deserve him?

When school let out, Dalmi, Jinhyeok and I went to hang out at Dalmi's boyfriend's hideout. Actually her boyfriend picked her up on his motorcycle, and Jinhyeok and I took the bus. A motorcycle fits only two people.

Dalmi's boyfriend lived in a shipping container. That was why it seemed appropriate to call it a hideout rather than his house. The place was thick with the scent of fabric softener. It smelled nice when you walked in but then, just thirty seconds later, you developed a pounding headache. Like your skull was being crushed. Should the home of a technical high school student smell like fabric softener? It felt wrong. When Jinhyeok and I arrived, Dalmi's boyfriend would pull out two mats and blankets. The frilly light-pink blankets had a sheen to them. Jinhyeok and I lay on one mat and Dalmi and her boyfriend lay on the other. The four of us lay there, making out with our partner. We just kissed earnestly, without chatting or joking or talking or being silly. Now that I think about it, that was weird as hell. What kind of double date is that? At the time, though, it didn't feel strange, it felt as natural as eating and shitting and sleeping.

How far did Dalmi and her boyfriend go? Did he touch her boobs? Did he touch her. . .down there? I didn't think they had sex. Because that was a dynamic act that I would detect even if I wanted to be blissfully ignorant. Which I didn't. But they were dead quiet. They couldn't be sleeping, could they? As for Jinhyeok and me, all we did was kiss. It didn't occur to me that there were other possibilities. Maybe it did to Jinhyeok. If one of our hands accidentally grazed a crucial body part, we flinched and moved it. We didn't hold each other. We didn't even hold hands. Only our lips and tongues touched. But it wasn't dull. I could make out for hours. The inside of Jinhyeok's mouth was so interesting, like a piece of land you wanted to learn everything about. Like a crossword puzzle. In the shipping container, time flowed, solid matter in liquid form. My lips began to ache. Everything smelled like spit. That smell, mixed with the pungent fabric softener, made me feel light-headed.

It was peaceful. If you took away the intense scent, that is. We were young but kissed chastely like seventy-year-olds. It was far from passionate and electric. It felt comfortable, languid. Nothing was lacking. I hope Jinhyeok felt the same. After a while, I would say goodbye to Dalmi and her boyfriend and leave the hideout to go post flyers. That was the life of a working woman. Not being able to do what I really wanted to do. Having to do what I didn't want in order to do what I wanted. I had to hustle to buy underwear from YES. Which makes me realize I definitely did think about the possibilities that lay ahead of just kissing.

Jinhyeok usually accompanied me. Starting at the top of a building, we went down one flight at a time. He would hold up a flyer and I would stick it on a door. He would cut tape in appropriate lengths and keep them at the ready on the tips of his fingers, then offer his hand whenever I needed one.

He was an excellent assistant. 'If you're gonna help me anyway, wouldn't it be faster if we split up?' I asked. I didn't say, *Then I'll be able to buy underwear sooner.* Jinhyeok laughed, and, between the fifteenth and fourteenth floors, held my hand in his own, taped, hand.

It was then that I began to work on a love journal. At a stationery store I bought a spring-bound notebook with a heart on the cover. The same place Dalmi and I had bought matching phone charms. For three hours I agonized, picking this and that item up, before finally deciding on a glittery pen, forty-eight coloured pencils and a gaudy, poorly constructed sheet of heart stickers. It cost me a fortune – five thousand won. That amounted to five hundred flyers. I carefully crumpled the first page of the notebook and wrote: *This is not trash. This is my pride that I threw away for you.*

I was very earnest.

There are so many cute animals in the world. A cockapoo, a cuckoo, and a kangaroo, too. What do I want to give you and only you? An Iloveyou.

You got a text from your wifey. Only four characters can be delivered because your phone is running out of space: LuvU.

Kissing fish don't survive the death of their mate. They die from loneliness or from starvation. Oh no! I've become a kissing fish! Because I can't live without you.

Time to get your cheating vaccine. Get it even if it hurts! You better get this shot and not cheat on me!

You won't be able to find the end of this thread. The day you find the end of this thread is the day you and I are done.

On sunny days I want to save a little sunshine in a glass bottle. So I can give it to you when you're having a bad day.

Testing you for colour blindness. Do you see the word Love *above? What? No? Then that means my love has blinded you!*

If you don't see a single star in the night sky, it's because I've taken all the stars. You know why? So I can give them all to you, the person I love.

Plastic doesn't break down for over a thousand years. So I put my love for you in plastic. So our love will stay the same even after a thousand years.

I wish my name was Iloveyou. Then every time you call me by my name, you would say you love me!

I was so very earnest.

Jinhyeok's name wasn't anywhere in my love journal. It was meant for him but I didn't write his name down. I left the space for his name blank. I already knew I was going to give it to someone else. Even though I hadn't met him yet.

I worked on my love journal during class. As I have explained, I knew I was going to end up at the vocational high school anyway, so I didn't need to study. In fact, it would be awkward if I did well in school, even by accident; I had to be bad at school. Otherwise, I knew I would feel cheated if I got good grades but couldn't go on to an academic high school because of Mum. I secretly drew in the journal when the teachers turned their backs to write on the blackboard. When they glanced my way I quickly slid it under my textbook. Much to my impatience, my work progressed slowly.

It might have been during Home Ec. while I was colouring in the kissing fish that I suddenly sensed that the classroom had turned way too quiet. I glanced up and saw my teacher looking down at my love journal. The entire class was holding their breath, watching us. Kids looked fearful and excited. They were all just waiting for me to get slapped across the face.

'You have a talent for drawing.' That was all she said as she went back to the front of the room. White noise filled the classroom as though the kids had been unmuted. Chairs creaked, pages flipped, kids murmured. *You have a talent for drawing.* Maybe that was her elegant way of disciplining me. I'm sure you don't need me to explain how I took that, a girl who had only heard one compliment her entire life, which was *You're so patient.* I heard the wheels of destiny whirring. From inside me. Years later, I would become an art school student volunteering to draw soccer balls on kids' faces during the World Cup. I would become a poor but happy person without any career prospects, someone with an ambiguous skill that wasn't all that useful in any given situation.

'Don't tell him.' My sister was referring to her husband.

We were in her apartment in Wirye New Town and I was trying to pay her back for what she had done for me years ago. For the first time in a while, I was making decent money from a subcontracted illustration job. You see, my sister had paid my hagwon fees when I was preparing for my art school applications as well as my college tuition. Mum was incensed when I announced that I wanted to be an artist. Dad – pfft. Let's not even go there. Despicably, my sister defended them. Claiming that Dad had lost confidence after his bout with bankruptcy during the IMF financial crisis and that Mum had simply accepted their own limits as parents. Pfft. When she got married, my sister lied to her husband about her finances, claiming she had a lot less. She did that to help our family monetarily, to sock away emergency funds. It sounded like she had concealed the fact that she had lent me money, too.

Gold balloons shaped like numbers hung on her living room wall. 9 0 0. I asked what they were for, and she said it had been nine hundred days since Seobin's birth. As if nine hundred days was something worth celebrating. It wasn't three hundred sixty-five days or a thousand days. Nine hundred? My sister's KakaoTalk profile noted *Seobin+900* and *Pancake-27*. Accompanied by a red heart. Every day, Seobin's number counted up and Pancake's counted down. I was envious of Seobin and Pancake, which was what we were calling the baby currently residing in her belly. I was envious that they had a mum who memorialized every day her children had been alive. For Seobin and Pancake, every day was their birthday. Every day was a celebration. I wished my sister was my mum. Mum didn't even know when I was born. Even when it mattered, she had trouble remembering the precise date. How did someone like my sister come from someone like Mum? It was shocking.

'Are you still itchy these days?' my sister asked.

'I'm basically becoming a crab.'

'Oh, I almost forgot,' she said, and went into the kitchen. Waddling, since she was so hugely pregnant. She put something into a Baskin-Robbins bag. She told me to take it.

'What is it?'

'Jerusalem artichoke tea. It's supposed to be good for your skin. It's anti-inflammatory. A doctor was talking about it on TV, that inflammation is bad for skin. They're teabags, so you just put it in hot water and steep. Is boiling water too much for you?' she suddenly snapped. 'What's wrong with you?'

'Why are you mad?'

'I'm not mad,' she said, mad. 'I'm not mad.'

'That's cute.'

My sister laughed almost reflexively. We would have killed each other by now if we didn't have *that's cute*. She rubbed her belly; maybe she could feel the baby move. Maybe Pancake had laughed.

'I've never heard of a Jerusalem artichoke. You can make tea out of artichokes?'

My sister was addicted to TV programmes about health. She went online to buy barley sprouts, aronia berry, psyllium husk and so on, all processed into pills or powders. There was not a single day that passed without a package being delivered to her door.

'It's not an artichoke.'

'So it's Jerusalem?'

My sister stared at me, fed up. 'It's like chrysanthemum root.'

'When I got tested for allergies, they said I'm highly sensitive to white daisy.'

'It's not white daisy, it's like chrysanthemum. Just drink it. Just do it.' She got mad again. 'You think I'd kill you? Stop arguing and just do what I say. Just drink it. You're so. . .'

'That's cute.'

A gold balloon fell off the wall. The 9. Of the 900. There was a 9 in my birthday, too. I touched the balloon. It made a squeaky sound.

Seobin woke up from her nap and toddled out. She already knew how to walk. She already knew how to talk, too. She already had teeth. It was creepy. Seobin picked something out of my hair. A cherry blossom petal. On my way to Wirye I had walked down a street lined with cherry trees; the petal must have fallen in my hair. Not a single petal could be found on the ground yesterday, the branches gripping tight to their precious flowers, but that wasn't the case today; it was pretty windy. The wind had rolled up behind me like a huge ball and shoved me along. My legs carried me even when I tried to stop. Petals swirled around me in a tornado. I remembered that a flower was a plant's genitals. Pedestrians looked happily up at the sky to take pictures of those genitals. Some trees already had green leaves clinging to their branches. In a month like April, yesterday and today could feel vastly different, and the same was true of today and tomorrow. It was April. My birthday was 9 April. Seobin was nine hundred days old.

'Happy birthday,' my sister said.

It was a good day for me to pay her back. It was my birthday, but truth be told it wasn't really the day I was born. Or maybe it was. This date hadn't been chosen out of malice. It just ended up happening. A coincidence. I remembered the goofy version of the 'Happy Birthday' song. *Why were you born, why were you born.* I took a bag of Haribo out of my pocket and held it out to Seobin, whose birthday was every day. Happy nine hundred days. Would a gummy this size be big enough to block the airway of an almost three-year-old? Just eat it. Stop arguing and just do it. You think I'd kill you? Really?

'Are you hungry?' My sister heaved herself up from the couch. She looked tired and heavy with Pancake. She looked like a pregnant woman. Maybe that was obvious. 'I can make you miyeok guk.'

'But you don't like it.' My sister had started disliking seaweed when she realized she had been brainwashed by that

49

clothing store lady, who had been instigated by Mum. At one point she did like it, but she grew to hate it. She had taken only a single sip that time I visited her in the boonies. Did she like it again now?

'I don't?'

'*You* have it. I'm going to go eat grilled beef.' I picked up my bag of Jerusalem artichoke tea. 'Thanks for paying my tuition back then. I'll keep it between us.'

I didn't say anything presumptuous, like how she shouldn't give or lend our parents any money. That she could tell our parents she had none to spare, like she had told her husband. What right did I have to tell her that? I wanted to tell her, *Use it for yourself, not for Mum or Dad or me. Not for Seobin or Pancake or your husband. Don't buy me Jerusalem artichokes. What are you thinking? Jerusalem artichokes?* When my sister told our parents that she would support me, I let her. I did that for her. She didn't know that, for me, it was still a big festering wound.

Seobin saw me off, holding the Haribo bag in one hand and the flower petal in the other.

4

At Onjo Junior High, the custom was to gift a box of Mon Cher cream cakes on someone's birthday. A box contained six cakes and cost around two thousand won. You could buy them at the cafeteria. Even if you weren't that close to someone, just friendly enough to say hi, you would give each other Mon Cher. 'Hey, it's my birthday today.' 'Oh yeah? Here's your Mon Cher.' It was similar to the congratulatory money you would give to newlyweds. What goes around comes around. Because our school had an insane number of kids, every single day was someone's birthday. Which was why I couldn't take even one day off from my job posting flyers.

It was 9 April. Cherry blossom petals were scattered in the hallway. Kids who had received or would receive Mon Cher from me gave me Mon Cher boxes. I stacked the boxes one by one on top of my locker until they nearly reached the ceiling. A new record. I got more than even Dalmi! While Dalmi received them, she didn't give any out – pretty girls could do that – so she got fewer gifts on her birthday. What Dalmi didn't know was that the Mon Cher boxes stacked all the way up to the ceiling were the fruits of my labour. Or maybe she didn't want to acknowledge it. She glanced up at the tower and said curtly, 'It's gonna fall, just put them in your locker.' Served her right. Of course I didn't put them in my locker. Display, not consumption, was the purpose of the Mon Cher boxes. A birthday marked an occasion to demonstrate who got the most Mon Cher and whose friendships were tighter. I was no longer who I used to be. I was best friends with Dalmi, I was going out with Jinhyeok from the main building and I got tons of Mon Cher. Oksu scurried past the lockers, her head ducked. I looked away from her. I was afraid my Mon Cher tower would fall. The abundance of cream cakes was the prize for pantsing Oksu behind the heavy purple velvet curtains.

The problem was how to transport all these boxes home. Makttungi Uncle came to pick me up after school. It was unavoidable. Makttungi Uncle was the only person I knew with a car. Thankfully he could come get me because business was slow at his failing restaurant. It was already taking a giant step toward its fateful decline. The problem lay in the amount of free food he'd given away at the opening celebration. Who in the world would pay money to eat something they had gotten for free?

'Hey, kiddo!' Makttungi Uncle rolled down the window of his Musso and waved.

We loaded the Mon Cher boxes in the back seat. I was a bit tense. I wanted him to be impressed. I wanted to shout, *I'm special, I'm someone who is showered with all these presents. I'm special, even though I wasn't before.* I suddenly thought about my grandma. Grandma was Makttungi Uncle's mum. Makttungi Uncle had a mum, too. That fact was always amazing to me. Later, Grandma would die from septicaemia caused by a bad post-vaccine reaction. Grandma was a terribly difficult patient. She was fretful, trying to rip off the respirator and the needles and all the equipment. She begged to be sent home. In the hospital they interpreted this to be a positive sign. 'She's still got strength,' they said, then put mitts over her hands and tied them to the bed railing. Grandma resisted for some time before giving up any hope of going back home. She didn't bang on the railing with her mitts or make it impossible for the other patients to sleep. Instead her eyes turned cloudy, unfocused. I felt bad for the hospital staff but I wanted Grandma to make a fuss. Grandma died in the midst of receiving all kinds of life-sustaining care. Even though she had signed a directive refusing life-sustaining care at the health centre when she was mentally with it. You see, as a formality, the doctors wanted a definitive answer from the family when she was slipping in and out of consciousness. My uncles objected. Mum and her sister couldn't persuade their brothers. So the torture continued. My sister couldn't go to the funeral because she was pregnant with Seobin. They said a pregnant woman couldn't attend a funeral because it would bring bad luck. My brother-in-law didn't, either. Or maybe it was because they weren't married yet. Grandma's body was wrapped in pink silk. The undertaker untied the ribbon to reveal Grandma's face. She looked completely normal. She didn't look dead. 'I love you, Mum,' sobbed Mum. 'I know you had it rough. Don't be sick over there, be well.' She wiped her eyes with a towel, which she had brought from home to sob into. Dad stood there quietly. By then, my parents had separated and were talking about divorce, but they were still married on paper. Which was why he was there. My aunt was crying, leaning on Mum's shoulder. Her husband said, 'Mother,' then got choked up and couldn't finish his sentence. A dozen cousins, all younger than me, sniffled. Did my two eldest uncles cry? I couldn't tell you because they were standing behind me. Their wives weren't there, as they had both got divorced. Only Makttungi Aunt was there, since she was still married to Makttungi Uncle. The only daughter-in-law. The undertaker bound Grandma's arms and legs together to put her in the coffin. Makttungi Uncle wailed, 'But my mum hates tight spaces.' I was shocked; it was the first time I had seen a grown man cry. The undertaker reassured Makttungi Uncle, saying, 'I'll take the ties off soon.' My eldest uncle, the chief mourner, wrote Grandma's name on the coffin. In case the coffins got mixed up in the crematorium. He had terrible handwriting.

After delivering my Mon Chers home, Makttungi Uncle went back to work in case any customers stopped by. Nobody was home. No clients with numbing cream and plastic wrap on their eyebrows. Did everyone go out together to look at the cherry blossoms? I opened the fridge to see if a birthday cake was in there but there wasn't. I kicked the boxes of Mon Cher into my room. Mon Chers without an audience had no meaning. They were useless.

My bed was empty. I used to share that bed with my sister. We slept in the same bed until she left home to go work in the boonies. She took the spot by the wall and I slept on the outside. She liked being cosy and I didn't like the feeling of being boxed in. After she left, I took over her spot against the wall. Now it was entirely my own bed, but I still only ever used half. You didn't lose your habit of sleeping in a narrow space. My shoulders were stiff from it every morning.

I lay among the Mon Chers that I had flung all across the room. I decided I was the lead in a spy movie. A spy wearing a tight, opalescent leather catsuit. I lay gingerly, avoiding boxes that would explode if touched. And then I sank into gloom. *Why were you born?* A centimetre-thick layer of dust covered the floor. I looked up at the bed. I reached out. I gently stroked the twin mattress. Unless I was a giant I wouldn't be able to reach all the way to my spot by the wall.

My phone buzzed. My sister. She was asking me to bring her some spring clothes. Ever since I visited her with my thermoses full of soup, she had been asking me to run errands for her. She had learned it wasn't impossible for me to get there. I shouldn't have encouraged this bad habit. I snapped my phone shut. Spring clothes? Are you serious? I'm thirteen now. Way too old to run your stupid errands. If I could be born again, I wanted to be the eldest. I wanted to make my little siblings do things for me. *Turn off the light. Bring me some water. Turn on the light.* Life would be so easy! Or else I wanted to be an only kid, like Dalmi. Did her taciturn mum buy her a cake for her birthday? Light candles? Did Dalmi get up from the table before her mum, even on her birthday?

I had to post flyers. I'd had to skip going to the hideout in order to bring all my gifts home. I missed the shipping container that smelled like fabric softener. I missed Jinhyeok's lips. What did Dalmi and her boyfriend do when Jinhyeok and I weren't there? Did they do it, finally? Did they moan as loud as they wanted? Her boyfriend would be shocked out of his mind if he knew that Dalmi put lip tint on her nipples and down there. I hadn't seen it myself, but I was sure Dalmi was tan everywhere. I didn't know why she put the lip tint on her knees. She said it made her look sexy but that didn't make sense to me. The MISSHA researcher who'd developed the lip tint would never have imagined that the product would be slicked not only on the lips but all over the body.

Dalmi didn't give me Mon Chers. Did that mean she did not want to be my friend anymore? No, our friendship was solid. I wasn't too worried. Jinhyeok had come over to the annexe to give me a single box of Mon Cher before going back to the main building. Did he want to break up with me? But I'm still his girlfriend. . .Would it be petty to give *him* a single box for *his* birthday? I suddenly wondered if Makttungi Uncle was back at the restaurant. Were the plants thriving? Was the baby in Makttungi Aunt's belly doing well? Earlier, when Makttungi Uncle was leaving, I told him sorry. It would have made more sense to say thank you. Idiot. I thrashed on the floor, pushing the boxes away. None of the Mon Chers exploded. My phone buzzed again.

I'll pay you ten thousand.

I got up and dug through her side of the closet.

After delivering my sister's clothes, I was walking along the dusty dirt road toward the bus stop when a black sedan drove by. A SsangYong Chairman. The silver trim around the car made me think of a killer whale. I knew that model well because Dad used to have one before his company went under. I finally reached the bus stop five minutes later. The Chairman was idling there. I opened the passenger door and got in.

'Hello, Assistant Director.'

I don't know why I got in the car. Because I was familiar with that car, having ridden in one as a child? Subconsciously? That wasn't really it. I just assumed we knew each other. But as soon as I got in the car, I realized I knew him but he didn't know who I was. I didn't know what to do, but then the assistant director said 'Hi' so naturally that I felt at ease. He must have been freaked out that a strange girl had just hopped into his car. I wanted to die of mortification. So stupid. In the side mirror, I spotted the bus pulling up. Only then did I hear the hazards blinking. Would he think I was weird if I got out now? Even though I had gotten in only a moment ago? My agony didn't last long. The assistant director started driving to make room for the bus.

'Doing an errand for your sister?' He was looking straight ahead.

I was taken aback. 'Do you know my sister?'

'Isn't she the bookkeeper?' murmured the assistant director, hesitant. Somehow the assistant director knew not only my sister but he also knew me, too. He said he'd seen me in the cafeteria and remembered me because I was eating food I'd brought. And that I looked like I had a bone to pick with the seaweed. And that my sister boasted about me often – so much that he had heard about me. And that, yes, he did recognize me, I must be the little sister.

I was amazed. Sure, yes, the cafeteria, but my sister bragging about me?

So I mentioned my sister's name to see if the person the assistant director was talking about was the same person as my sister. And it was. Apparently, I was known in the boonies as a good girl who studied hard. I thought I was going to pass out from the sheer horror. I despised my sister for saying such things. None of them knew about my slutty way of sitting cross-legged on top of the lockers. None of them knew I made out with Jinhyeok every day at the hideout. None of them knew I had to go to a vocational high school and become a bookkeeper like my sister. That I had to follow Mum's blueprint. Everyone at my sister's work would laugh at me if I ended up getting a job there myself. They would tut at me, pityingly.

'Don't be too angry with your sister,' the assistant director said, breaking the silence.

Could he hear my thoughts? My heart nearly stopped. I'd have to knock on my chest to see if my heart was still safely in there.

'I know it's annoying to have to do errands. I was the youngest in my family so I had to do my share, too. She just wants to see you. She probably wanted to give you some pocket money, too. She probably felt awkward just giving it to you so she made you do an errand.'

'Oh, I see,' I said modestly. For now, I told myself, act like a good girl. Whether I wanted to or not, since that was how I was known around these parts. I refrained from thinking about anything, just in case the assistant director could really read my inner thoughts.

'What are you doing?' he asked.

I realized that my phone charm beads, shaped like bears, like gummies, were in my mouth. I must have been sucking on them. I did this whenever I was happy or anxious. My phone charm that matched Dalmi's. The gummies that never melted. Light yellow, but sometimes rainbow-coloured. Light refracting through them, resting between Dalmi's nose and mouth, before skittering off to the corner of the wall. Did they glow inside my mouth, too?

I quickly spat them out along with a long string of saliva that I wiped on my uniform skirt.

'Just getting some air,' I said.

The assistant director lowered the window to let the

breeze in. I got some air. It was comforting and tepid. Neither cold nor warm. The air caressed my cheek. I felt understood. The people in the boonies didn't know that the dean had slapped me across the face.

I could feel the assistant director glancing over at me.

'What is that?' he asked.

'It's a bear-shaped, gummy-shaped. . .' How could I describe what this was? I was annoyed, confused by my limitation. I was near tears. 'It's a phone charm but it's shaped like bears, like gummies. . .'

'Oh, like Haribo.'

I accidentally dropped my phone between my seat and the door. I fished it out. 'What's Haribo?'

'German gummies.' His tone wasn't condescending. There was nothing the assistant director didn't know about. He wasn't even boastful of that fact. He wasn't like anyone else I knew. Not like Mum or Dad or my sister or Dalmi or Dalmi's boyfriend or Jinhyeok or my English teacher or my Home Ec. teacher or the clothing store lady or the dean of students or Makttungi Uncle or anyone.

Flower petals threw themselves silently onto the windshield. The cherry blossom petals were weightless. They drifted away. Cherry trees flanked the street on either side. They continued all the way down, right to the vanishing point. We were cocooned in a pink tunnel. It reminded me of the adventure-filled hallway of the annexe at school. The hallway lined with metal lockers. The hallway where the weird girl crapped and snakes came down into the school and the dean of students roamed around, slapping his pool cue against his thigh. I wanted my life to be gentler than it was. I thought about Oksu scurrying past the lockers. About her naked body in the auditorium. I got mad whenever I thought about her. People got mad when they felt bad. I didn't want to be like that. I didn't want to be the kind of person who apologized and asked for forgiveness just because they felt bad. That was shameful. For me to be ashamed or for me to be mad? Flower petals floated in through the open window. They collected on the floor.

'You were born on such a nice day,' the assistant director said, brushing the flower petals off his head.

It was that day that I heard something earth-shattering, cataclysmic. That I was pretty. At first I thought the assistant director was talking about the cherry blossoms. But he wasn't. I seized up as though cold water had been thrown on me. I was insulted. This was worse than slapping me across the face. I'm pretty? Me?

'No,' the assistant director corrected. 'I didn't say you were pretty.'

Well, that made more sense then. I must have lost my mind. I had clearly heard something that hadn't been directed at me. It was an insane thing to hear. I had obviously gone mad. I was losing my mind. *Crazy bitch! You're a crazy bitch!* You can be a crazy bitch but I can't? Dalmi can be pretty but I can't?

'I didn't say you were pretty. I said you look pretty.'

What's the difference? I wondered. I knew I wasn't pretty, I knew that I had a conscience, but what was the difference? I became a little desperate. The assistant director explained the difference. 'You're pretty' was a value judgment, he said, and 'you look pretty' was a factual statement. Which meant I was factually pretty! I was beginning to feel more elated than when the Mon Cher tower had reached the ceiling. I tried to calm my somersaulting heart but it wasn't easy. My heart wanted to run around the hallway, shrieking. For the first time in my life, I had been told that I was pretty. Well, that I looked pretty. Me, who had only heard the halfhearted compliment *You're so patient.* And, of course, according to my Home Ec. teacher, I *had a talent for drawing.* My passion for drawing withered in an instant. As though it had never existed in the first place. Girls who looked pretty didn't have to draw well! They could go to a vocational high school. It didn't matter how they lived their lives. They weren't outcasts even if they didn't try to be on everyone's good side. They received mountains of Mon Cher even if they didn't make any effort at all, even if they didn't work posting flyers to buy everyone else Mon Chers.

The Chairman pulled up in front of my house. The assistant director had seen me home. I had been 'escorted' home. We'd arrived home before I could fully savour the assistant director's statement of fact. It had taken me forever to get home on the bus before but it was so much faster by car. Which was unfair. I unfastened my seatbelt and checked to see if I had everything. The ten-thousand-won bill my sister gave me for bringing her clothes, and my phone and little bits of trash in my pockets, like my gum wrapper – after all, I'm a model citizen who never litters – and a bus pass – I'm good at drawing but I don't forge my bus pass like the other kids – and coins – this is money I earn by walking down the stairs of a full apartment building. Coins were easy to drop, so I checked this and that coin again, dragging my feet, expanding time. While the assistant director waited patiently.

All of a sudden I was terrified. I dug up that old feeling of fear inside me. I was afraid that the front door would be locked. That when the door opened, with someone unlocking the door from the inside, it would be smoky and yet smell delicious. *You've been brainwashed. To like seaweed. They think it's a waste to feed you beef. That is the kind of people they are.* But wasn't it okay to eat seaweed today since it was my birthday? Not that much time had passed since I had been forced to eat up all the soup made with the mounds of seaweed I had soaked. I had to eat the soup for every single meal, I had just shoved it down. That was the punishment Mum had come up with. I didn't necessarily think it was unfair. I should be punished for doing something stupid. Maybe I should have eaten the soup a little slower, though. I was afraid I would find miyeok guk if I looked inside a pot in the kitchen. And I was afraid that there wouldn't be any miyeok guk. What would be less horrible? I didn't cry when I was sad, only when I was confused. I remembered my first kiss, with Dalmi. I remembered the steamed egg that Dalmi's mum had made in the microwave. I could hear the dishes being washed around the corner. We were reflected in the TV screen, leaning against each other like a house of cards. Rainbow light darting this way and that. That bitch Dalmi. You can't use people. Nobody should use anyone. I wasn't born to provoke the boys pining after you. I wasn't born to make your life easier. I look pretty. I'm special.

I fussed with the window of the Chairman, opening and closing it. I didn't want to get out. And the assistant director didn't tell me to get out. He didn't say, *Here we are.* It smelled like 'cool water' in the car. That typical male scent. A blue scent. Makttungi Uncle smelled like this, too. I knew it well.

It wasn't Dad's scent. Dad, who was so obsessed with Mum, used her lotion instead. This was the scent of cool water. But cool water smells different than cold water. Everyone thinks of the same smell when you say 'cool water'. A blue smell. What it smells like in a men's bath or the gym shower.

Was I scratching my arm in the Chairman? I don't remember. I do remember other things.

I loved terrible memories. I was obsessed with misfortune. I collected awful memories inside the keepsake box in my heart. I was in love with bad habits.

The assistant director lived in an apartment paid for by the company while he was working here. That was incredibly cool. Even though he seemed embarrassed by it. It was messy because it was a temporary residence; there was no other reason. Not because he was lazy or because he was a slob. It just wasn't his real home and there was no point in keeping it neat. A button-down was flung over the back of a kitchen chair. Just a single man's rental unit.

Strictly speaking, he wasn't single. A clever little boy named Dongo was in the living room slash kitchen slash office, intently playing a computer game. There were two monitors before him, alongside a laptop. The setup reminded me of a spaceship's controls. Dongo was the assistant director's son. 'I heard he's gay,' my sister had said at the cafeteria. Could gay people have kids? Weren't babies made from sperm and an egg? Nobody else was in the apartment.

While the assistant director made dinner, I hung out with Dongo. He taught me how to play StarCraft. His chosen race was the Zerg.

'Pick the Overlord, Nuna,' he said.

'Why?'

'Because then you can do recon. The map gets brighter wherever the Overlord goes.'

The Overlord flitted away like jellyfish. It was so gross that I nearly gagged.

Dongo asked me if I wanted to change races. 'There's also Terrans and Protoss.'

I picked Terrans because their colour reminded me of Dalmi's cell phone. These Terrans were silver and blue cyborgs, and looked the most like humans. I'd only ever been interested in humans. Protoss looked like moths and Zergs looked like bloodied organs.

'Pick the SCV, Nuna.'

'Why?'

'Because you can dig for minerals.'

I picked the SCV. Now it felt like I was just working. I didn't want to work.

'I'll do this part for you.' Dongo grabbed the mouse out of my hand. 'You can do the fun stuff. Like fighting. I'll let you know when it's time to attack.'

I liked Dongo. He was a dependable kid, more grown up than anyone I knew. I watched him dig for minerals. In between digging he added troops, building up his unit. They looked strong.

'Guess what? I've met Lim Yo-hwan,' Dongo bragged, his hand moving nimbly.

'Who's Lim Yo-hwan?'

'A pro gamer. He plays as Terrans. You like Terrans, right?'

'Where did you meet. . .' I couldn't remember his name.

'Lim Yo-hwan.'

'Right, Lim Yo-hwan. Where did you meet him? Does he live around here?'

Dongo stared at me in disgust. 'On Battlenet.'

'Battlenet?'

'It's where you can play StarCraft with other people. Like online.'

I pointed at our enemies, the Protoss. 'So these are other people, too?'

'No, that's the computer. You're still a beginner so you have to start by playing against the computer. Anyway, I met him. What do you mean, how did I know? Because his ID was SlayerS_' 'BoxeR'.' Dongo typed in the chat box: ARE YOU YOHWAN? 'That's what I asked. You have to ask in English because you can't type in Korean.'

'And?'

'He didn't answer.'

'So did you win or lose?'

Dongo sighed dramatically. 'Of course I lost. How could I win against Lim Yo-hwan?' He pushed the mouse toward me. 'It's your turn. Quick!'

I held my breath. I was so nervous. I was scared I might die. A person wasn't behind the Protoss, I knew that it was just the computer, but I was still fighting a war. Why were we fighting, anyway?

'It's okay if you die. You can just play again,' Dongo told me.

His encouragement boosted my spirits and I destroyed the Protoss. Maybe I *was* having a good time. The Terrans lost. A plane flew over and destroyed our troops. Buildings crumbled and units melted. Dongo pretended he didn't care.

'Why don't we have a plane?' My question came out like

a critique. I hadn't really been all that invested, but now that we lost, it upset me. 'Why not?' I hounded Dongo.

'I don't know how to do that yet.' Dongo confessed that he lost every single time he played, that the plane flew over and destroyed his troops every single time. But he still kept playing. He kept loading StarCraft and logging on to Battlenet.

'Then what's the point?'

'Because it's fun even when I lose.'

While Dongo was in the bathroom, I quit StarCraft. I clicked randomly on the folders on the desktop. There were boring Excel and Word files. What did the assistant director do again? He was in the audit department? I looked for a layoff list to see if my sister's name was on it but I didn't see anything about work. Only meaningless numbers. Did he play the stock market? I opened a folder and in it was another one. I opened that, and found another. Like a Russian nesting doll, it was just layers of folders. Maybe something important was hiding inside. Porn? I really wanted to check if he was gay. If he was gay, he would only watch porn with men in it. If not, if he was into women, they probably would have huge racks. I kept digging into the folders. Dongo came out of the bathroom and the assistant director called, 'Time to eat, kids!' I quickly closed all the windows.

The button-down had been removed from the kitchen chair. Dongo and I sat next to each other, across from the assistant director. I was always eating with other people's families. Dalmi's mum must have been so annoyed. She had to make steamed egg for a complete stranger. *You think food is free?* Mum's food wasn't free but Dalmi's mum's was. I couldn't figure out how the world worked. It was all so unfair. Did the love for your children become standardized, too? As in, if one mum loved her child a ton, did that mean another mum loved her child exactly that much less? Did Mum make Dad pay for his food, too? The kitchen in this apartment was filled with smoke, and the range hood whirred. It smelled so familiar.

'Are you crying?' Dongo looked at me with concern.

I shook my head. I swiped my eyes with my sleeve. I picked up a piece of beef and put it in my mouth.

The assistant director looked ill at ease. 'Maybe I should have made miyeok guk.'

'No!' I shouted, without realizing I was.

Startled, Dongo dropped his chopsticks.

'I'm sorry, no, I'm not sorry. No, I'm sorry,' I babbled.

'It's okay,' the assistant director said. He lowered his gaze to the table, maybe in an attempt to give me some space. He ate quietly.

I was grateful that he didn't ask me what was wrong. If he did, I might have sobbed. I would have become the biggest burden a person could be to another person. My ruffled feelings settled as his calm voice said, 'It's okay.' My clogged throat widened back to its normal size. Dongo patted me on the back cautiously, in a way the assistant director couldn't see. His hand was gentle. I could smell seawater in my nose.

5

'What's wrong?' Jinhyeok asked, pulling his lips off mine.

We were at the hideout, under the shiny pink blanket. His question broke the unwritten rule that we did not speak. I could smell his breath. I couldn't hear Dalmi or her boyfriend. What the hell were they up to? What nasty stuff were they doing, all quiet like that?

'What?' I snapped, breaking the unwritten rule myself.

'What are you thinking about?'

I was annoyed. But I had to wrap it all up in something nice. I had to pretend I didn't know what he was talking about. 'You.'

We started making out again. But I couldn't focus. I would move my lips and my tongue, but when I paid attention I would discover that they had stopped moving. Jinhyeok was making all sorts of useless moves on his own. His tongue groped mine like tentacles. Gross. It prickled and hurt. It didn't feel like enough. I wanted something else. How had I been able to do this for hours on end? Should I let him touch my boobs? No, I couldn't do that. He would just dump me immediately after.

Afterwards, Jinhyeok didn't come along when I had to go to work. So petty.

I rode the elevator to the top of an apartment building and trudged down the stairs, flight by flight, pasting flyers on doors. My knees ached. *Going out of business sale. Everything must go! The owner's gone mad!* Apparently the owner was going mad constantly, advertising these sales the entire time I had this job.

I didn't feel like working. I could make more by running errands for my sister. I could get ten thousand for a single trip to the boonies. Why should I have to toil and sweat like this? I texted my sister out of my precious allotment of texts. It was an investment of sorts. 'Don't you need summer clothes?' No answer. She used to text me back immediately. But after the assistant director was deployed from headquarters, the staff in the boonies had to pretend to work hard. They tried to show that they had good attitudes. The school commissioner's visit was just a single day, but the assistant director was staying on for some time. I felt for them.

I went up to the owner who went mad, the husband of Mum's client, to return the remaining flyers. 'I'll do the rest tomorrow,' I told him. But he turned suspicious, wondering if I'd thrown away a few of the flyers. I probably should have. I walked all the way to town. Coins in my pocket weighed my skirt down. Today was TwoTwo, Jinhyeok and my twenty-two-day anniversary, so I had collected two hundred won from each of my classmates. I had to reveal our secret romance in order to do so. Like the Mon Chers we exchanged on birthdays, we gave each other two hundred won for TwoTwos. Sometimes, though, it was abused by older students. Even if we didn't know each other they would come over and demand two hundred won. *I swear*, they would say, *It really is our TwoTwo.* Somehow it was always someone's TwoTwo. Maybe they were all two-timing or even eight-timing each other.

THE CRUSTACEAN

The cherry trees along the street were green and pink, half flowers, half leaves. It had poured the day before, causing many of the blossoms to fall. Blossoms and leaves could be together on a single tree, but they could never bloom in the same spot at the same time; leaves sprouted only after the flowers faded away. I spotted kids wearing Onjo uniforms, the one we wore between seasons. I think they now call them spring and fall uniforms? Which was just the uniform without the blazer. We wore white blouses and grey skirts and grey checkered vests. The check pattern had a little bit of dusky brown-red mixed into it. The neckties too were a dull red. Now that it was getting warmer, we didn't have to wear the horrible red-bean blazers. A silver lining.

I got to the YES store. I went in to check out the lingerie sets. I acted like a picky shopper, holding this one up and then another. Goodbye, polka dots! But my excitement faded when I thought about showing them off to Jinhyeok. I selected a white lace set that I thought would make me look innocent. Or perhaps it would make me look like I was wearing a diaper? The salesclerk urged me to buy it, telling me it was the most popular design. 'Let's see,' she said, eyeing my boobs under my vest, then picked up the same design in an A cup. It made me miserable. Even though I was miserable, no, *because* I was miserable, I still bought the lingerie set.

With the YES shopping bag dangling from my wrist, I crossed the street and entered MISSHA to buy the lip tint. Which one did Dalmi use again? It was 3,300 won. I didn't have enough. I pictured myself stealing it. The clerk was organizing a display. All I had to do was slip it into my pocket when she wasn't looking. I flinched and put the tint down. I could have stolen it but I wasn't certain that I actually wanted

71

to steal it. I wasn't sure I wanted to be that ballsy. If you looked pretty, could you steal the tint? Dalmi must have stolen it. But Dalmi was pretty. Dalmi was pretty but I looked pretty. A factual statement. I was agonizing over this when an older lady handed me a broom. 'Why don't you sweep the floor?' she asked, perhaps having mistaken me for someone who worked there. A few cherry blossom petals were scattered on the floor. The wind must have blown them in when the door opened or they must have fallen off a customer's head or shoulders. I did as I was told and swept the floor.

Beauty is the highest virtue. I left MISSHA without the tint. It was actually harder to be bad to the bone than to be a goody two-shoes. I'd just borrow it from Dalmi. If I put on my lips what Dalmi put down there, wasn't that like an indirect kiss? Indirect. . .oral? I got goosebumps on my arms. It seems strange now, but back then we all shared makeup. Back then we were less concerned about hygiene. We even borrowed circle contact lenses from each other. Everyone kept getting eye infections. It turned out to be a good excuse to leave school early, so sometimes we volunteered to be infected. I sound like an old lady saying all this, and it's only been twenty years. Recently each day has felt vaguely familiar, as though I'm living the past at the same time as the present. Time is flowing side by side, with what happened twenty years ago layered over the present. It's torture. As torturous as trying to stop scratching myself. Maybe my memories are what's irritating my skin. I get the feeling that I'm living too much of life, all at once.

Not everything has a root cause. I mentioned earlier that the last doctor I saw at Boramae Medical Centre had told me that. I made another appointment but cancelled it soon after. I would try living with my skin. All I had to do was not scratch, do nothing and just stay still. Why couldn't I do this very simple thing? Going to the doctor was expensive, too. And I'd just paid back my sister for my college tuition. All these years after graduating, I still didn't even have health insurance. Health insurance was like your lunar birthday, like key-money loans – strictly for adults. I didn't even have a credit card. The bank wouldn't issue me one. Even though I was a diligent taxpayer. Though taxes are for anyone alive, not just adults. 'Do you have proof of income?' asked the teller. 'What's that?' I asked. With the teller's help I managed to access a document on the National Tax Service app. It showed my income: one million seventy thousand won, the paltry sum I made that year, rather than a month. The teller said in a roundabout way that my application would be denied because I was a freelancer, not because I was dirt-poor. I felt bad for taking up the teller's time. My situation didn't alarm me. I don't care about money. I actually feel anxious if the number in my bank account grows. But was I making bad choices? I only worked when I needed to. I don't want to live my life to the fullest. 'What?' scoffed my sister. 'You don't care about money? That means you're obsessed with it.'

The agency emailed me, asking me to send in revisions. They had already finalized everything and I had been paid for my work, but they reached out right before going to print. Their client must have had last-minute demands. The agency was a subcontractor, and I was their subcontractor. I had illustrated an educational comic book for children. It was about Chiruchiru and Michiru – no, wait, that was the

Japanese pronunciation that we Koreans had adopted, too – it was about Tyltyl and Mytyl, who went on an adventure and learned about all kinds of things. The agency said, *It's great, but it's a little confusing. It makes sense for Mytyl, but why is even Tyltyl in polka dots? Is it an homage to Yayoi Kusama? What if we take out the polka dots? Otherwise it feels like it's too much. And why is this rainbow in the background? Are rainbows visible at night? And why are all the eyebrows blue?* Et cetera, et cetera. They weren't going to compensate me for the extra work.

Finally I sought another dermatologist. Two weeks after cancelling my appointment at Boramae Medical Centre. I had gone to this small practice at the very beginning, when my symptoms hadn't been too bad. This doctor wasn't a specialist but I couldn't bring myself to make another appointment at Boramae Medical Centre and wait another few months. The doctor welcomed me, saying it had been a long time. That put me on guard; shouldn't they hope that a patient never came back? Since coming to the doctor would mean I wasn't well? But I was a client. Doctors couldn't make money if everyone was healthy.

'I tried to live with the itchiness but it's not really working.' I didn't confess that I had seen other doctors, in case I hurt this one's feelings. My sister would have said to me, *Why are you worrying about the doctor? Worry about yourself first.*

The doctor said that itchiness wasn't something you could just live with. 'You can't force yourself to be okay with it,' the doctor said. He looked excited for some reason. Like he was soliciting potential customers on the street.

'Well, I can just stop scratching,' I said crankily. I wanted to refute whatever the doctor said. 'I can just stay still. I can just stop scratching.'

According to the doctor, the human brain didn't understand denial. Being told not to think about elephants meant you ended up thinking only about elephants. 'There's no need to suffer,' the doctor said. 'The moment you stop thinking you have to ride it out will probably be the moment you're fully cured.'

'But a crab wouldn't feel itchy, right?' Me and my big mouth. This wasn't something I could resist just because I wanted to. *Grow up*. My sister's voice rang in my ears. *What is wrong with you?*

'Oh, do you like crab? It *is* blue crab season. The females are at their peak in the spring, and the males in the fall. Do you know how to tell them apart? If the pattern on the stomach looks like a phallus, it's a male, and if it looks like breasts, it's a female.' The doctor flipped through my chart. I had gotten tested for allergies here. The specialists I'd seen later had said allergy tests were meaningless. 'You aren't that sensitive to crab. You do need to be careful around white daisy and mugwort.'

I didn't correct the doctor's misunderstanding. I didn't double down, saying, *A crab wouldn't know what it feels to be itchy, right? I didn't say, Because their skin is bone. I'll just ride it out. No, I won't think about how I'll just ride it out. I just won't think about how I won't think about how I'll just ride it out.* Instead, I asked, 'What about Jerusalem artichoke?'

We drew straws for our seat assignments and I got to sit with Dalmi. I was actually assigned elsewhere but I bought the seat next to Dalmi from the kid who had drawn it. Capitalism rocks. Stupid capitalism. Dalmi got to sit next to me for free. I suggested we split the cost evenly, five hundred won each, but she refused. 'Why should I?'

Right. There's no reason for you to chip in. Because you're pretty. Was the assistant director lying when he told me I looked pretty? He didn't seem like a liar. What would he gain by lying to a little kid? I mean, I wasn't such a little kid anymore. I was thirteen. And on the evening of my birthday, the assistant director drove me home and abruptly left. Like he was a taxi driver. He didn't even ask for my number. Though why would he?

Now that we were sitting side by side, Dalmi and I could write notes to each other without having to pass them. A thousand won for that privilege was a good deal. I scribbled a note to her in a blank spot in my math textbook. *Can I borrow your tint for a day?*

Why?

At least she didn't say, *Why should I?*

I racked my brain. Why did I need the tint? Because I had to sleep with Jinhyeok? Because it was about time? Because we just celebrated our TwoTwo? Shouldn't I wait until we'd been together for a hundred days, at least? I remembered the stories of girls giving it up and getting dumped right after. What if he did the same thing to me? Should I really be sleeping with a guy who'd only given me a single box of Mon Cher? It wasn't like he was buying me grilled beef. But I didn't want to sleep with the assistant director.

I propped my elbows on my desk and gripped my head. That was when Dalmi handed me the tint. The MISSHA tint she always kept in her vest pocket. The 'cherry blossom' colour. The flower was the genitals of a plant, I remembered.

Dalmi used this on her lips and her knees and her nipples and her own genitals.

As the math teacher turned to the blackboard to solve a linear equation, I quickly scrawled with my ballpoint pen, *What did you guys do at the hideout? The day we didn't go.*

Jinhyeok and I hadn't gone to the hideout on my birthday. Dalmi wrote something with her Pilot Hi-Tec, which was considered a luxury item at Onjo. It was like a name-brand purse. It made yours seem worthless.

We slept together.

I gazed at that word, devastated. So that's what had happened. Just like I thought. They were just waiting for the day we didn't tag along. Did it hurt? Did she bleed? My heart was shredding. Dalmi was my first kiss. I felt heartbroken. If Dalmi slept with her boyfriend, that meant I had to do the same with Jinhyeok. I had to catch up. I really didn't want to, though. Not the sex part; the sex-with-Jinhyeok part. I wasn't really working myself to the bone, saving money, *for him*. I didn't endure the humiliation at YES to buy the lingerie set *for him*. I suddenly remembered a laxative ad. *Saramdeureun modu byeonhanabwa.* A pun: *Maybe everyone changes*, which also sounded like *Maybe everyone has bowel movements*. I was the one who had changed, not Jinhyeok. He had done nothing wrong.

Dalmi picked another coloured pen from her pencil case and wrote something else:

We slept together. You know he works the night shift at the gas station. He has to nap so he can work.

That was it? That was all that had happened? Did he buy her these fancy pens, too? I suddenly thought of the Chairman. I wasn't in my right mind.

Everything must go! The owner's gone mad!

That day, I didn't go to the hideout after school. It felt wrong to be making out with Jinhyeok while Dalmi's boyfriend napped so he could get enough rest before work. And what did Dalmi do, while her boyfriend slept? Apparently she just gazed at his face. The Dalmi I knew wasn't a romantic, she was a sexpot. So what was going on? It was a mystery.

Jinhyeok got mad at me again.

I went home after pasting flyers. Mum was jabbing a vibrating electric needle into the eyebrows of a client. Dad held the needle while Mum dabbed at her work with a kitchen towel. When Mum held out her hand, he swapped the towel with the needle. Like a nurse handing a scalpel to the surgeon. *Scalpel! Suction!* The other neighbourhood women were sitting around, peeling apples to snack on. Everyone's eyebrows looked identically stencilled. Of course they did; the same person had drawn them in. Did Mum have a talent for drawing when she was my age? Was that how she had fallen into this line of work? The women chatted among themselves, which was how I learned where my parents had been on my birthday. They were at the opening of an adults-only game room owned by the husband of one of the women in our living room. Apparently it was doing really well. Maybe that guy could hire me? Maybe I could post ads for a gambling den. Then I'd be arrested and the cops would storm my classroom and drag me away in handcuffs. Strangely I liked that possibility. But seeing as I was already incarcerated in Onjo Prison – how could I be arrested again?

I walked into my bedroom, the one I used to share with my sister, the floor so dusty that I used the Mon Cher boxes as stepping stones. They crumpled under my weight and the individually packaged cakes inside burst. The soles of my feet tickled. I tore open a box and shook it upside down to get everything out, then I took off my polka-dot panties, cut them up with a pair of craft scissors and hid them inside the box. Mum would kill me if she found out. What I really wanted to do was set fire to the storage room full of panties. But you had to start somewhere. I felt a tiny bit better as I put on my new lingerie set. I squirmed into it carefully, wanting to keep it looking untouched and new.

Oh! The lip tint! I carefully peeled off the underwear and was about to apply the red tip to my nipples, but paused. What if it got the tint on my bra? Maybe I shouldn't have bought it in white. No matter how virginal it looked, it would be a complete bust if the tint was smeared on the important parts. So, I applied it to my lips and my knees. I understood why you'd put it on your lips, but the knees? Dalmi said it was sexy, so I trusted her. I didn't want to admit it but I was a fervent Dalmi believer. I vowed to stop thinking about her. But as soon as I made that vow, she was all I could think about. I wished I could colour in my nipples and between my legs with the lip tint. Why was only my face so red? Wasn't my nickname Hongikingan? Maybe I would turn red if I was boiled. I twisted this way and that to check the fit of the bra. The A cups were way too big. I could slide an entire fist between my chest and the fabric. I should have bought the bra in a different colour. I didn't think they would let me return it now as I had already worn it. . .

Whatcha doin? Jinhyeok texted. I didn't respond. I had to save my texts. For whom? I wasn't sure. This was just one of thousands, tens of thousands of things that confused me.

Why did I borrow the lip tint and why did I buy the lingerie set? For whom? For what?

I hid the Mon Cher box containing my shredded polka-dot panties under my bed. Mum would never find it there. She wasn't the kind of mum who searched under her child's bed. And Dad – pfft, let's not even go there. Mum didn't pay attention to me and Dad didn't pay attention to the fact that he didn't pay attention to me. Later on, all grown up, I become so ballsy that I revealed on my sister's wedding day how upset he'd made me, to his face. At the time Dad was at risk of being left by Mum. Divorce was gaining steam among people their age. But Mum kept putting it off, saying, 'I'll do it after your sister gets married,' 'after Seobin is born,' 'after Pancake is born.' As though she enjoyed making Dad squirm. Or maybe she was worried about him. According to her, Dad was the kind of person who would sign the divorce papers and then immediately go kill himself. Even so, she went everywhere with the divorce papers on her person. As was the case at my sister's wedding. It should be noted that Seobin was already present at the wedding, concealed under her wedding dress. Which was why she and her husband hadn't come to Grandma's funeral. Her wedding dress had a bell-shaped skirt so she could hide Seobin. When Mum got up from her seat to light candles as part of the ceremony, she left her hard embroidered handbag on her seat. The divorce papers were carefully folded inside. They went everywhere with her but she never deployed them. At the reception I quickly got between my parents, as they weren't getting along. With Mum, I ganged up on Dad. Two on one. Just like how Sein and Dalmi ganged up on me. Mum was of course a bad mum, but Dad was a bad dad and he was also a weak man. Which was way worse. I berated him and he ended up in tears. Even though he had failed to drop a single tear during his own mother-in-law's funeral. He cried his heart out at the wedding reception, using me as an excuse. It was the first time since Makttungi Uncle sobbed at my grandma's funeral that I saw another adult man crying audibly. Only people who had done terrible things cried like that. I figured Makttungi Uncle should have been a better son while his mother was alive if he was going to cry at her funeral like that.

Anyway, back to my thirteen-year-old self. I put my school uniform over my white lingerie set. I didn't really have anything else to wear so it didn't make much sense to change out of my uniform. Food wasn't free, and neither were clothes. I wished the clothing store lady had paid for her eyebrows with clothes instead of those polka-dot panties. That was wishful thinking. I was already in junior high; I was all grown up. All the clothing she sold was children's clothes, and they were all too small for me anyway. Though they probably could have fit across my chest.

I walked out the front door and through the yard, past the single cherry tree dotted with blossoms and leaves. Pink and green. I pushed open the gate. My feet moved forward on their own. Like they were responding to a beat I couldn't hear. Similar to how I had found the Haribo charm in my mouth when the assistant director asked me, 'What are you doing?' Like the way the breeze had entered through the open window just as I said, 'Just getting some air.'

It was then that I saw the Chairman parked in front of the gate.

6

My name is Chichirim. Before, I was Hongikingan, but then, around the time green started threading through the pink canopy of the cherry tree, I became Chichirim thanks to the assistant director. I thought about the story of Chiruchiru's blue bird. Why wasn't my name Chichibird? Why was it Chichirim? The first *Chi* must be from Chiruchiru, the boy, and the second *chi* must be from Michiru, the girl, and the chichibird had to be the bird the two siblings were looking at. And *rim* – meaning forest – being the woods where the chichibird lived. I instantly put the meaning together. The name Chichirim had been waiting patiently for the right person to come along. Waiting for me. The instant I heard the name Chichirim, I fell in love with myself. A girl with a pretty name deserved to be loved.

Honestly, my real name was too ordinary. If someone called it out loud at school, ten of us turned our heads in unison. It could even be a boy's name. The worst. My gender-neutral name had to be why my chest was so flat. And it was why I wasn't convinced I was a girl. My parents must have pulled my name out of a hat – that's how little they could be bothered. That was the kind of people they were. I wanted a cool name like Dalmi. I wanted to be at the top of the social pyramid. I didn't want to be ostracized again. That was why I complained about my life to the assistant director at Kimbap

Paradise, where we went after he picked me up that afternoon; acting like a petulant child, I even lisped in an effort to be cutesy. I would have been murdered if I acted like this at home.

'Chichirim.' By giving me my name then and there, the assistant director swiftly dispelled my complaints. You remember the poem 'Flower' by Kim Chunsu? The one that's in all the Korean textbooks? The one that's about how being called by your name makes you significant, meaningful to the person calling you that name? And just like that, when he called me Chichirim, that was who I became.

Once upon a time, back in elementary school, before I had anything of my own, before I even had pocket money, my friends would go to Kimbap Paradise after school for tteokbokki and other snacks. I would wait for them outside. Sein, who would later become Dalmi's henchwoman and ostracize me, would sit elegantly inside with two other girls. They would invite me to come inside and eat, wasn't that so nice of them? I was too proud and pretended I couldn't hear them. With the tip of my sneaker I traced an image of tteokbokki on the ground. I must have liked to draw back then, too. Maybe I wouldn't have been ostracized if I'd gone inside when my friends kept waving at me to come in. Who knows? I pretended I didn't see them beckoning but I was about to go in, feigning reluctance, when the food came out. They buried their faces in the dish, chowing down. Fine, whatever. Anyway, that memory was why I chose to go to Kimbap Paradise with the assistant director. Now I could go there as often as I wanted. I could thumb my nose at Sein. But Kimbap Paradise wasn't paradise for the assistant director; it was just a cheap snack bar that made him ask, 'Are you sure that's where you want to go?'

Earlier that day, when I'd left the house under a spell of some kind, the Chairman had been right there. The passenger door was three steps away. Like he had purposely parked his car right there. So I would only have to walk three steps, and three steps only. I opened the door and settled into the seat, just as smoothly as I had at the bus stop in the boonies.

Dongo wasn't at the apartment. He was subject to his parents' custodial arrangement. He was with his dad Monday through Wednesday, and he was with his mum Thursday through Sunday. The life of a kid with divorced parents. My birthday a few days ago had fallen on a Wednesday. That must have been why Dongo was there. Wednesday was the day Dongo left to go to his mum's place, his real home. The day the assistant director had made his son something delicious to eat, so the boy could go to his real home and brag about how great his dad was. I shook that thought away to protect what the dinner of grilled beef had meant to me. It was corrosive to have a victim mentality. To describe what had happened not through value judgment but factual statement: the assistant director hadn't bought the beef for me. It had already been there, in his fridge. We didn't even know each other the day before my birthday. I mean, we knew *of* each other, but we hadn't met yet. My visit to his apartment had been unplanned, caused by a series of harrowing events. . .Of course, the assistant director might have wanted to place a delicious morsel of food in my mouth. And it just so happened that he had beef, perfect for grilling, in his fridge. It was all the same whether he had gone out and bought beef because he wanted to feed me, or he had wanted to feed me and happened to have beef in the fridge.

The desire to feed me was the same in both scenarios. *That* was a value judgment.

The assistant director went to take a shower, saying he had to wash after work because there was a lot of dust blowing around in the boonies. I listened to the water running as I sat at the computer desk with its many monitors. I turned on StarCraft. What race should I pick today? I missed Dongo, so I chose Zergs even though they were disgusting. I sent Overlords around to brighten up the map. They floated around but couldn't attack. I dug for minerals. I remembered the cheat code Dongo told me about. SHOW ME THE MONEY. Now the numbers flipped rapidly, making me dizzy. I could build as much as I wanted to. I could build up my units. But then I lost to the Terrans. Their air unit attacked and destroyed my headquarters.

I logged on to Battlenet. I wanted to fight against someone real, not the computer. I wanted to get destroyed by someone real. I was matched up against Zergs. But I was a Zerg, too. I guess you could fight your own race? Maybe that much was obvious. Was that just the natural order of things? My opponent seemed to be a beginner. We played for quite some time. After all, a fight between two weak parties tended to be fiercer. I attacked the enemy camp. I killed units, I demolished buildings. Then I felt bad. I chatted, ARE YOU OKAY? ARE YOU ALRIGHT? It felt like I was asking myself this instead. My opponent didn't answer. The war was vicious. I became more tense, revved up. Maybe I could even win. Though I wasn't sure I wanted to. If I won, I would tell Dongo. Would he be proud or hurt? A message popped up in the chat. OKAY. Another one: GO ON.

It's okay, go on.

In the end, I lost. I wrote GG for Good Game, the proverbial white towel thrown into the ring. Feeling refreshed, I exited Battlenet and closed StarCraft. I started poking around on the desktop. Or rather, I headed straight to the folder that had opened up like a Russian nesting doll. I finally got to a folder of photos, organized by year. My chest tightened. Maybe I had played StarCraft to delay this moment of discovery. I opened a folder at random. Thousands of pictures filled the screen.

I couldn't believe my eyes. Didn't I just turn off StarCraft? Everything in the pictures was the colour of Zergs. I blinked. This wasn't StarCraft. This wasn't a game. This was all real. The folder contained picture upon picture of corpses. Corpses of a variety of ages, a variety of killing methods, a variety of stages of physical damage. A veritable corpse expo.

The cursor was trembling onscreen. I yanked my shaking hand off the mouse. I spat the phone charms shaped like bears, shaped like gummies, out of my mouth. The ones the assistant director had told me looked like Haribo. I guess even murderers liked Haribo. I was in a murderer's lair. Dongo must have been a pawn to keep me blissfully unaware. Because everyone let their guard down around kids and animals, didn't they? A criminal often keeps a family portrait as the wallpaper of his phone to make sure his victims are relaxed. He couldn't kill me last Wednesday because Dongo was present. Even murderers had sons. Because of his custody agreement, he killed only between Thursday and Sunday. And today? Well, today was Friday.

It was too quiet. I was getting the sense of déjà vu. When had I felt like this before? Right, right, I had felt like this during Home Ec. I was decorating my love journal below my textbook while the teacher wrote on the blackboard. The love journal I was making for Jinhyeok. The love journal I hadn't written his name in. *You have a talent for drawing.* This was, of course, before I'd met the assistant director. But I'd already known whose name would be written in the journal. I had remembered the future. Now, I looked up and saw the assistant director gazing down at me. Water dripped from his hair, dampening my grey skirt. It was cold. Cool water.

Grey is the colour most vulnerable to water.

7

Grandma passed away. My sister got married. Seobin was born. Pancake was conceived. Makttungi Uncle's restaurant went under. I paid my sister back. Mum and Dad didn't get a divorce. I know what happened to my family, events both small and large, because I wasn't murdered at thirteen. I'm now in my mid-thirties.

That day, after it was all over, the assistant director explained everything to me. That he collected pictures of corpses whenever he felt depressed. That he felt relief when he saw damaged bodies. *Liar! You're a murderer! The worst liar!* I ran to the computer and opened the Russian nesting doll folder. I checked the year on the first folder. I guessed what the assistant director's age might be. The year on that first folder was a long time before he was born. So the collection of corpse pictures was merely a disgusting habit. . .I felt a surge of disappointment. Then I thought, this man is hurting. We are the same race. We aren't Terrans. I too held a keepsake box in my heart in which I collected bad memories. Once, I'd opened it and showed Sein. I'd taken out a memory, put it on my palm and carefully held it out to her. We had been playing at the playground when I did that, out of the blue, because in that moment I was happy. And I couldn't stand being happy. So I had to sacrifice Sein. Innocent Sein gazed studiously at my unhappiness. 'Ew,' she said. *Ew.* After that, Sein became

Dalmi's henchwoman and I was ostracized. I'd paid dearly for my mistake. I didn't blame Dalmi. I loved her. I blamed Sein. I blamed myself. Usually a fight between two weak parties tended to be fiercer.

OKAY. GO ON.

There were specific rules I had to follow while having sex with the assistant director. No questions were allowed. That was a difficult rule to follow because I didn't know how to speak without using the word *why*.

'Why, why, why, all you ask is why!' my sister would groan, fed up. Once Seobin learned to talk, she was deluged by *whys*. But she didn't scold Seobin. Because a child was supposed to ask questions.

I quickly got used to the assistant director's rule of not asking questions. I got used to the absence of *whys*. Things got easier, less confusing, once the *whys* went away. He saved me from my avalanche of *whys*. The only thing I was allowed to say was 'I'm sorry'. I'm sorry. I liked that more. Because I wanted to apologize and say I was wrong. I wanted to say I was sorry. I wanted to ask for forgiveness. And I wanted to forgive.

As the drops of water landed on my grey skirt, I looked down. They resembled drops of blood. This was what it looked like when my period leaked. Obviously, whoever designed our uniforms knew nothing about the female body. *Hey, you have something on your skirt.* We would take our red-bean-porridge-coloured blazers off and tie them around each other's waists. That's what we called 'bonding'. So nice. The girl who ties a blazer around a friend's waist today strips a classmate naked tomorrow. To bond. I remembered Oksu's naked body. I remembered her kinky pubic hair. I thought: I don't mind dying.

'Get up.' The assistant director's voice was arid, lacking all emotion, neither cold nor hot, just like a spring breeze.

I felt understood. I got up.

He sat on the couch. I followed his orders and took my clothes off. I was in my white lace bra and panties I had bought at YES. My lips and knees were the colour of cherry blossoms. From the lip tint I had borrowed from Dalmi. Because I couldn't steal it and instead had obediently swept up the flower petals before leaving the shop.

Beauty is the highest virtue. My armpits and legs were bare. I had used Dad's razor. Dad was always puzzled by how frequently the blades dulled. The razor wasn't free. I hadn't shaved my pubes, worried they would get stuck in the blades, worried I would seem like a slut. I had to seem inept, inexperienced. In the same vein, I'd heard that you shouldn't raise your butt when a guy pulled your underwear off. Though I hadn't known I would be taking my panties off myself until this very moment. Would I be a decent corpse? A corpse that looked pretty? I knew my picture would be added to the Russian nesting doll folder. It had been so obvious that the folder was concealing something. That was the assistant director's mistake, his error. If he had left the folder in question out there on the desktop, I would never have clicked on it.

Under the assistant director's orders, I moved toward the couch. I was not allowed to ask why. I felt unburdened from my need to understand. *Whys* only ate away at you. He was fully clothed. I kneeled so his pants were before my eyes. I lowered his zipper. I was doing what I was told but I wanted to do it before I died. I refused to go without having had sex. Otherwise I would be missing out. Otherwise I would end up roaming this life as an unhappy spirit. I didn't want to end up a virgin ghost. Dalmi had said she'd been in bed with her napping boyfriend because he had to go to work at night. Dalmi had just watched him sleeping. Was Dalmi a virgin? I wanted to be more experienced than Dalmi. These circumstances led to my holding the assistant director's penis in my mouth. He didn't take any of his clothes off. But his penis was visible. I was fully naked, kneeling on the floor. His penis was bumpy. The doctor who circumcised him must have had poor stitching skills.

The tip of his penis jabbed the back of my throat and made my eyes water. He ordered me to raise my head, his voice still flat. I spat his penis out to look up. But somehow I was now looking at the floor. I felt woozy, like the time I lost consciousness when a swing hit the back of my head. That had happened in elementary school, during field day. I had been walking down the field, but when I opened my eyes again I was looking at dirt. I had come to on my own; nobody had woken me up. I was a loner so nobody had been with me. The swing must have hit me on the back of the head. Or maybe not. I had gone to the nurse's office, mobbed by kids with a range of minor injuries. Those idiots were wailing over silly little cuts. 'I passed out,' I announced to the nurse. She'd checked the back of my head and told me I could go. I didn't have a visible injury. Losing consciousness was an easy way to keep living, because time flowed even when you were knocked out. Meanwhile, when you were conscious, you risked being in pain. I had left her office satisfied. I hadn't been able to get the nurse to care, but I was still pleased that a small part of my life had gone by at no cost.

Now, I was staring at the wooden floor of the assistant director's apartment, as I cupped my hand against my throbbing cheek. Maybe I didn't pass out. Maybe I was slapped. The assistant director didn't rub his cheek against mine, he didn't ask, *Why would I hit you?* He wasn't the dean of students. He wasn't like anyone else in my life. Mum didn't hit me. Neither did Dad. Because they didn't love me enough. Parents use corporal punishment out of love. Some even consider it a parental duty. He hit me. Which meant he must love me.

He taught me to raise my head with his penis still in my mouth. He taught me to meet his eyes with mine. My eyes welled with tears from being jabbed in the back of my throat, which warped his face. Weren't we supposed to kiss first?

You hold hands, then you hug, then you kiss, then he touches your boobs and then you touch each other, and finally you have sex. But this was a progression different from what I had thought would happen. Then again, Jinhyeok kissed me before he ever held my hand. Guys must just ignore the correct steps. Then again, this wasn't a relationship; he was a murderer.

'I'm sorry.' My words were garbled; there was no room in my mouth.

He grabbed me by the hair and yanked my head back and forth. I felt sick. Would he hit me if I threw up? I wanted him to hit me. Being conscious meant being in pain, but if you were in a ton of pain, it paralyzed your consciousness. Like passing out. At least during the time you were being beaten, you would be free from painful thoughts. Which meant you could live life for free, without any effort. Pain was painful but a ton of pain ended up being pleasurable. The way scalding water feels cold. Cold water. Cool water. A salty fishy bitter liquid spurted down my throat. I swallowed. He stroked my head kindly, ever so kindly.

'Good job,' he said.

It was all Dalmi's fault. And the matching cell phone charms we'd bought together. It was all because of the beads, shaped like bears, shaped like gummies. All because of the seaweed I had been brainwashed into believing I liked. All because of my sister, who was the one who informed me I was brainwashed. On 9 April, on my thirteenth birthday, the assistant director watched me suck on my phone charm in his car as we drove away from the boonies. Instead of imagining Haribo in their place, he imagined his penis. At his apartment, when I burst into tears at the sight of the grilled beef, he thought I looked pretty when I cried. Not a factual statement but a value judgment. This pretty-looking girl is pretty, too. So instead of asking, *What's wrong?* he said, 'It's okay.' He dropped his gaze to the table. 'It's okay to cry. Go ahead.' He actually wanted to make me cry. Especially when I had tears welling in my eyes from being jabbed in the back of the throat with his penis.

Dongo was the reason he escorted me all the way to my house from the boonies – though we ended up at his place after all – while he plotted what would happen next. Dongo was at the apartment. His mum hadn't yet picked him up to take him back to his real home. Dongo still had to play video games and eat dinner. The grilled beef wasn't for Dongo; it was for me. The assistant director said that a pretty-looking girl had to eat something delicious. This, he explained, was how the world worked. He had realized something in front of my house, as I played with the coins in my pocket. *I guess I bought that beef to feed her.* He hadn't known that when he picked it up at the grocery store. Dongo took after his mum and didn't particularly like beef. He didn't like the taste of blood. Even when he ate fish, he only liked the ones that weren't too fishy. Now I understood why Dongo had just picked at his food. I had assumed he had lost his appetite out of worry for me. The kid had patted me gently on the back. That grilled beef was just like my love journal with the blank space for the recipient's name. We had wanted each other before we even met. We had both known that. Well, we hadn't actually known we wanted each other, but we had known that we were meant to want each other. We knew we would end up sitting side by side in his car at the bus stop. It had just been a feeling and it had come true. Deeply moved, I covered my mouth with my hand, and the assistant director added that he'd wanted to put things other than grilled beef in my mouth. He'd wanted it to hold other things. He said he wanted to stab me in the back of my throat. He'd wanted to come in my mouth. He told me it had tortured him not being able to because Dongo had been there.

I didn't scowl in disgust. This was a confession of sorts. He was wooing me. I understood him, the way the lukewarm breeze wafting in through the open car window had understood me, the way I had been understood without being told so. I understood him deep in my bones. As though our nerves were intertwined. We were the same species. We were Zergs. We were disgusting. We collected horrible things in our keepsake boxes. We took them out every day and polished them so dust wouldn't settle on them. I had sensed that he was different from all the others because he was the same as me.

He was me.

He zipped up his pants. I wanted to help but he looked so stern, as though he was saying, *How dare you*. The loving caresses were over, that brief moment of sweetness after a long period of pain. Bitterness enhanced sweetness. Like chocolate. It's over, I thought, and regret rushed in alongside relief. These feelings caught me by surprise. Was oral sex considered sex? Was I still a virgin? I remembered hearing about a woman who only had anal sex so she could insist she was a virgin. If your hymen was intact, did that make you a virgin? My knees throbbed. They were very red. The floor had pressed marks into them. Oh, so that's why you put tint on your knees. Reddened knees suggested sex. It would have a similar effect to my sitting cross-legged on the lockers. It was seductive. I should buy some tint myself. I should go to MISSHA. Wait, no, I won't be able to as I'm going to die here.

'Go over to the bed.'

We were in the living room slash kitchen slash office. I didn't need to wander around looking for the bed because there was only one other room. He wouldn't need to slap me again for me to understand. I went into the bedroom and stood in front of the bed. I didn't lie down because he had said, 'Go over to the bed,' not *lie down on it*. I was slowly getting used to his way of communicating. The corporal punishment of love was certainly effective. I wondered if he was going to kill me here. What if my blood gets on the blanket? Wasn't it better to die in the bathroom? It would be easier to clean up after me. Maybe he was planning to kill me later. After he had his way with me, like a kid gleefully tearing the wings off a dragonfly before killing it. Pain still loomed ahead of me. I was glad. I didn't like my life but I did want to live a little longer. Just a little bit more. He made me want to live. That's love, isn't it?

I only lay on the bed when the assistant director ordered me to. From now on I'll stop telling you *the assistant director ordered me to* because by now you probably understand that everything I did was based on orders. I was a slave, a marionette controlled by a psycho pervert killer. At this point, he still hadn't explained why he had saved pictures of corpses on his computer; he hadn't tried to charm me back yet. Instead, he hit me when I moved toward the wall without his permission. 'I'm sorry,' I said. I wriggled back to the edge of the bed where he could see me better. But he didn't touch me. I wriggled again, turning to lie parallel to the pillow. The mattress was a wide twin, not wide enough for me to lie that way, so I had to keep my knees pointed up to the ceiling. Still on my back, I turned to look into his eyes. If I didn't look into his eyes I got in trouble. He sat on a stool. He didn't touch me or himself. He just watched, his face blank. I sucked on my right forefinger and middle finger to make them spitty. With my left hand I touched my nipple and with my spitty right fingers I touched myself down there. Oh, I forgot to mention – he told me he preferred small kid boobs. He told me he found even an A cup too big. He was turned off by that. He explained it made him 'impotent'. 'What's impotent?' I asked. 'I can't get hard.' Did Dongo's mum also have a flat chest? I didn't ask. I didn't want to be more alluring by having a flatter chest. It made me happy that I was his type, but it still made me depressed. I should explain to you that the rule of not asking questions was in effect only during sex. It was fine for me to ask *why* at other times. In fact, it was more than fine; he thought it was adorable. I got the sense that I would become addicted to sex because I didn't like the word *why*.

Back to the scene where I was still lying across the bed. I put my middle finger into my vagina. Imagining it was his penis, following his orders. I followed his orders faithfully. I'd never before put a finger in my vagina. It was the first time I had touched the inside of my vagina. I was thinking about what it felt like. There were ridges just inside, like wrinkles, and it felt cushiony. Why did guys finger girls? It wasn't like your finger felt amazing. Did they like seeing the girl liking it? Did they think they were doing the girl a favour? Then why did guys finger sleeping girls? Right, he told me to imagine it was his penis. I focused again on how my vagina felt, not my finger. I'd only ever masturbated by crossing my legs and squeezing them together. I wasn't taught that technique; I had just been doing it since I was little. I had mastered the technique after intensive training. I could get myself off in ten seconds. But this, this didn't feel great, flailing my finger around inside my damp cushion. Why did I have to do this? It didn't feel good. And this couldn't be making the assistant director feel good.

But perhaps he was enjoying it. His face was still blank but it was redder. I braced my other fingers against where my thigh met my butt and made my middle finger go in and out. Then I pushed my ring finger in, too. I twisted my nipple with my left hand, like I was mushing eraser bits together. Did this feel good? It was like when I played dodgeball during PE. At first I didn't want to do it, but when I actually started playing, it was fun and I ended up giving it my all. I could hear the squeals of sneakers on the court. I could feel the cool air of the gym. I couldn't believe I was feeling pleasure right now. It was gross, horrible. Sein would be shocked out of her mind if I told her any of this. *Ew*, she would say.

I turned over and lay face down, continuing what I was doing with my hands. I wrenched my neck to the side, looking back at the assistant director. I opened my knees and raised my butt. I made a woeful expression, like I was about to cry. Tears could well but not flow down. That wasn't something he had already taught me. It wasn't something he ordered me to do. I had understood this on my own, based on his reaction.

He then tied my wrists behind my back. My centre of gravity shifted and I tilted forward. Whatever was binding my wrists behind my back was hard and made a series of clicks. Maybe they were cable ties. Now I'm going to die, I thought. I felt something trickling down my inner thigh. He licked it. I let out a short exhale. I nearly made a sound but I clenched my lips together so he wouldn't hit me again. I had learned not to say anything other than *I'm sorry*. He didn't seem to care. His tongue was gentle. It drew circles on the smallest, most sensitive spot. There was barely any pressure; it moved lightly, only grazing the surface. *What if I smell?* I worried even in the face of death. Even though I would smell even worse once I became a corpse.

I closed my eyes because I couldn't see his face anymore. My legs shook and electricity shot up my back. Something fizzy was running down my spine. I had to pee. My wrists hurt; maybe the cable ties were digging into them. I gripped my hands together as though in prayer. Every time my body twitched he warned me that I wasn't allowed to enjoy it. 'I'm sorry,' I begged. I tried to numb myself but it wasn't easy. This was completely different from the kisses I'd shared with Jinhyeok, the kiss I'd had with Dalmi. I realized I had wanted this feeling, I realized I had been missing this deep down in my bones, even though I had never experienced it before. The fact that I wasn't allowed to enjoy it made me focus on how much I enjoyed it.

I heard his zipper lowering and his clothing rustling. Still standing, he entered me while I was bent over. Unexpectedly, deeply. Lights flashed before my eyes. I was being stabbed. My body was being split in half. I was being torn apart. I felt paralyzed. I was paralyzed, but the sensations were clear; they were steady, piercing. He put a hand under my stomach and raised me up higher. He went in and out aggressively, spitting insults. 'Shut up, you whore. You bitch!' The bed springs made a racket. He slung his left knee on the mattress, balancing his right foot on the floor. He leaned on the bed and grabbed me by the throat with his other hand. I couldn't breathe. 'I'm sorry,' I begged. 'Please don't kill me.' I didn't want to die. I wanted to live a little longer. I wanted to live. I wanted to say all that but I could only cough. He loosened his grip on my throat to let me take a breath. Then he choked me again. I sucked in as much air as I could each time I was allowed to breathe.

Was I dead? Was this the afterlife? Still lying on my stomach, I looked around. Nothing was different. Was the grim reaper running late? Handling other important matters? I didn't know how you got to heaven. Did I need a ticket? Did I need a passport? I was worried about Mum and Dad. They were good people. Maybe I shouldn't have died. I was only ostracized once, what was the big deal? What did it matter that I had to go to a vocational high school? I could have looked back on all that fondly, with a smile. Time would have healed everything.

'Because I came earlier,' he said by way of excuse. He was grappling with his limp penis. Only afterwards did I learn that he suffered from psychogenic erectile dysfunction. But I didn't know that as I lay on the bed on an angle, looking out the window. Cable ties still bound my hands. Phew. I wasn't dead. I was glad but also somewhat disappointed. My parents went back to being bad people. Well, I'm going to die later, I reassured myself. It would be better to be killed in the bathroom, as I had originally thought. Then he could just wash it all away. Red blood sprayed on white tile would swirl down the drain. My god, erectile dysfunction? Was it okay to pity a murderer? When had the sun set? I hadn't noticed the time pass. It was dark outside but bright inside, thanks to the fluorescent lights. Like squid boats floating in the night sea. I should check my phone. If there's a worried text from Mum, I'll ask him to spare my life. I remembered a children's song I loved when I was little. *My dad, looking all around for me while I play on a rainbow hill.* Dad? Looking for me? As if.

With a snap, my arms fell limply to the bed. He had cut the cable ties with kitchen shears. I was free. I sat up and rotated my shoulders. My hands were dark red, my circulation cut off. Was it over? Even though he didn't come? Well, he did on the couch earlier. I felt bad. It must be because of my small boobs. It was my fault. Who would like a flat chest? This must be the first time he was experiencing the shame of going soft. He must feel so flustered. I wanted to say, *I'm sorry.*

But were we having sex right now? He seemed to like hearing that only during sex. Would I be putting more pressure on him if I said I'm sorry?

It had hurt. I hadn't gotten anything out of it. Everything ached below but I wanted more. He lay on the bed. This was new. The first time, he had sat on the couch while I kneeled on the floor. The second time, I was face down on the bed while he stood. Finally, we were sharing the same piece of furniture for the first time. It felt new. I lay next to him. I glanced down. He was hard again.

We made love the normal way. The way lovers did. I lay comfortably on my back with him above me. He moved gently and at a uniform speed like waves on a calm day. We did it with the lights off and under the blankets. This was how you were supposed to have sex. It was dark, but not dark enough to be scary. This man wasn't a murderer. I was certain of that. We kissed and held hands. I was happy. My tears trickled into my ears. 'I love you' sounded muffled, like we were underwater.

8

Happiness and misfortune took a placement test and were assigned to the same class for standardization. Or maybe the misfortune that soon swept over my family categorized my experience with the assistant director as happiness by default. Maybe our house wouldn't have been put up for auction if I hadn't felt pleasure during my first sexual experience, which had ended peacefully despite its violent beginnings.

I got out of the passenger seat of the Chairman and took three steps to open the front gate. I walked across the yard and yanked open our dented front door to see a red tag on every piece of furniture. I could tell instinctively that they indicated seizure. It was near midnight. It was after business hours but the blue-eyebrow brigade was all there. Saying things like, *I had a bad feeling about it, what did I say, didn't I say he seemed like a snake? We should have known when he opened up that gambling shop. A rag doesn't become a towel just because you wash it.* The ladies looked like they were having a grand old time. Like they had found something exciting to spice up their tedious lives. Maybe they were relieved that the misfortune had settled over us instead of over their own homes. They hadn't acted as guarantors. We were the only ones who had been conned.

'I saw these on TV!' Mum shouted, filming the red tags with her phone.

Dad looked at her lovingly, with a gentle smile on his face. Had the shock made him go mad?

We had managed to hold on to the house even during the IMF financial crisis, and now we were about to lose it. What happened was this: Mum or Dad, or maybe both of them, had acted as guarantors for the couple running the gambling business. That couple had been customers and neighbours, good friends, so my parents hadn't suspected a thing. The two couples had gotten to know each other at various gatherings and outings, going to see flowers blooming in the spring, joining hiking excursions, picnics, gye meetings, couples' gatherings and more. But the owners had gone bankrupt and vanished. Meanwhile they still had outstanding debts. And who was on the hook for them? Us. Why? Because my parents were their guarantors. Our possessions were seized. Our house was destined for the auction block.

'Oh, there you are!' The clothing store lady spotted me. Her husband was the one who had owned the Ssangbangwool factory. The main culprit behind my life veering into a ditch.

'Hello,' I said.

'Oh, honey, this is not the time for hello,' she said, and the other ladies burst into peals of laughter.

A bedroom door flew open. I nearly died of shock. Because it was the door to my room. I mean, our room. My sister came out and let out a howl. She slumped to the floor and began thrashing, spinning and kicking like a cockroach on its back. I brought her a cup of water to calm her down. She took a single sip, as she always did, and handed it back to me. Then she began thrashing again. I went to the sink to wash the cup.

*

The blue-eyebrow brigade went home. After her tantrum, my sister went back into our dusty room. I went with her. The floor was so dirty that we had to escape to the safety of the bed. The room was a total sty; nobody treated it like they owned it. Both of us were insane clean freaks when it came to our bodies, but we never cleaned the room. Because it wasn't my room. It was *our* room. Mum and Dad considered our room to be a black hole. As though it didn't exist. Crushed Mon Cher boxes were scattered all across the floor. Dust bunnies rolled around. Only the bed was clean, a pretty cosmos blossom amid all the neglect. My sister's spot was by the wall and mine was on the edge. I sat on the bed and leaned against the wall. Order was there to be destroyed.

My sister stared at my wrists. 'Where were you?'

I hid my wrists behind my back. They were ringed with cable tie marks. She's on the assistant director's team, I realized in an instant. And today, I'd had crazy sex with my sister's boss. Three times in a row! Him hitting me and coming, me being hit and putting it in my mouth and sucking and coming and edging closer and closer to death. The commissioner of the boonies, the rock star of the boonies, the celebrity of the boonies – he loves me.

'Getting some air.' My answer was bratty because I missed being hit, but my sister wasn't the type to dirty her own hands. She beat people up with words.

She studied my face. 'Did someone hit you?'

'Yeah.'

'Who?'

'The dean of students.'

'Why?'

'Because I was getting some air.'

'Why?'

'What do you mean, why?'

'Why were you getting air?'

'Why can't I get some air?'

Our conversation was stuck at the *whys* like overlapping mirror images. A hellscape of questions. I wanted to order her – *No more questions.*

'What are we going to do?' I dipped my feet back into hell.

'About what?' My sister joined me, too.

'About the house.'

My sister yanked her hands through her hair, huffing in exasperation. 'Why are you asking me that?'

'Then who would I ask?' Only then did I realize I didn't care at all about this problem. I didn't care if this stupid house was sold off at auction. I actually found myself hoping it would get sold. I wanted our family to shatter so I could go live with the assistant director. I wanted to play StarCraft with Dongo and have sex with the assistant director and eat grilled beef together and live in harmony, just the three of us. Or maybe I could ask Dalmi's mum to adopt me. Dalmi and I could be sisters. It would be fun to live in a female household. Or else I could try staying at Dalmi's boyfriend's hideout. There was room there since he worked nights at the gas station. Or I could just get married to Jinhyeok if none of those other options worked out.

My sister pushed me toward the outer edge of the bed. She lay on her side, facing the wall.

In the end, I opted for the last, probably easiest, option: get married to Jinhyeok.

Let's assume there are ten apples. The most delicious is

the first one and the grossest is the tenth. Someone who starts with the first apple gets to eat a good apple each time. First you eat the best apple, then the next best, then the next best. But if you start with the tenth apple, you eat a less gross one each time. First the grossest, then the next grossest, then the next grossest. I was the kind of person who always started with the tenth apple.

My night with the assistant director also played a part in my decision to sleep with Jinhyeok. I wanted to see if that violence was universal to sex. And the assistant director's preference for small boobs gave me courage. After school, Jinhyeok and I headed into town. I told Dalmi and her boyfriend that we couldn't go to the hideout today, that my boss wanted me to come early to get a start on the flyers. I told them Jinhyeok was coming with me to help. This was a white lie, like saying, *I was late because of traffic.* Social niceties that everybody trotted out all the time. Dalmi's boyfriend waved at us. 'Okay, good luck.' Dalmi smirked. They rode off on his motorcycle, out the school gates. I laughed to myself. I used to be envious, but now I was derisive. Those guys had never been in a Chairman, had they?

At present, I couldn't even afford to take the bus. I had to save my tickets because of my family's financial situation. So we walked all the way into town. It wasn't that far. It was nice out, too. Jinhyeok looked nervous. Because we had decided to go to a video room. *Wanna go to a video room?* was the same thing as saying, *Wanna have sex?* It would cost a pretty penny but it would be better than doing it at my future in-laws' place.

'Do some flips for me?' I asked at the top of the stairs leading down to the establishment.

Jinhyeok pretended he didn't hear me.

We went downstairs into the basement. This place must not have seen the light since the Big Bang a hundred million years ago. Darkness reigned, light was absent. It was spooky and musty. Minors weren't allowed in but the place was owned by the family of a kid in Jinhyeok's class, so we knew we could get in. The owner's son manned the counter after school. Of course, we picked a horror flick. Not on the pretext that we could cuddle, as we were already beyond that phase; instead I was planning to mask our moans as screams of terror.

Because we had an in, we were led to a nice corner room. We sat beside each other on the vinyl sofa dotted with cigarette burns. I was by the wall and Jinhyeok was on the outside. So he could protect me if a ghost popped up from under the sofa. The projector illuminated the dust floating in the air. The movie began as Jinhyeok fumbled around.

We began the way we always did. Kissing was easy. We had done this every single day at the hideout. Tense music piped in from the speakers. It got tenser, then stopped entirely. The ghost must be faking us out. Jinhyeok wasn't progressing fast enough so I helped him out. I pulled his hand onto my chest. My uniform vest was like armour around my small chest. He handled my boobs like he was studiously kneading dough; I didn't feel anything. I was exasperated but stayed put. I had to make it look like it was my first time. He sucked on my neck, panting. He undid the buttons of my vest. I cheered him on in my head.

It's okay. Go on.

He began to pull out my shirt tail from under my skirt; it was a big, long blouse, which I'd bought through school, so he had to pull it out for quite some time. His hand finally wormed its way under the shirt and undid my bra clasp. I stopped him right before my cup size was revealed. 'I'm not sure,' I said coyly. Perhaps let down, Jinhyeok moved away for a moment and pretended to watch the movie. Then he made another attempt at my boobs. This time I let him. Pushing him away once should be enough, right? He held my nipple like he wanted to pinch it off. Perhaps he was struggling to moderate his strength or maybe he did it because there was nothing to touch other than my nipple. His hand burrowed under my skirt to take my panties off. I made sure not to raise my butt. He touched me down there in the most annoying way. His nails were too long and dirty. I had clocked them earlier, when we were choosing the movie. The assistant director kept *his* nails clipped really short.

Jinhyeok paused his kneading. 'Do you ever change your underwear?'

'Hm?'

'Why do you always wear the same underwear?'

What was he talking about? *Why do you always?* As if he's seen my underwear before. *I have thousands of these damned panties at my house*, I wanted to say. That's when I remembered my bad habit, which I'd stopped a while ago. Sitting cross-legged on the lockers. He'd probably come by the annexe and seen it for himself if he hadn't heard the rumours in the main building. Bad rumours, I'm sure. *That weird girl shat on the floor. A snake came down from the hills. That ugly girl shows everyone her underwear.* One of the blue-eyebrowed ladies had said, *A rag doesn't become a towel just because you wash it.* This had to be the only reason someone like me could have a boyfriend. A boyfriend? Me? I was insane for thinking otherwise.

The ugly girl doesn't even get to eat the tenth, the worst, apple. That's the logic of this world. I was thoroughly demoralized after our visit to the video room. My appetite and motivation were gone. I no longer had a reason to keep living. When I thought of the assistant director, I felt only resentment. Out of nowhere he had to tell me that I looked pretty, planting false hope in my heart. In math class, the teacher made a terrible pun, saying, 'Know your value,' and I flinched.

The assistant director didn't call me. He didn't know my number. Was this what life was like for adults? On Friday, we'd made love for the first time, afterwards he'd brought me all the way home. As soon as the Chairman drove off, I realized we hadn't exchanged numbers. The weekend went by. Monday, Tuesday and Wednesday were his days with Dongo. On Thursday I hovered anxiously near the front gate, but the Chairman didn't come. Same on Friday. And Saturday. And Sunday. Monday was when Dongo returned to the assistant director's apartment. On Tuesday, Dongo stayed over. On Wednesday, Dongo went back to his mum. Thursday again. No car in front of the gate. I did all kinds of things under my blankets while thinking about the assistant director.

Nobody bid for our house. The blue-eyebrow brigade had flexed their power. Their network was enormous; their warning of blowback if anyone made a bid was effective. As though they had read out a declaration that bidders would be subject to boycott, picketing, ostracism and even a physical brawl. For the time being, we managed to stay off the streets. But it was for the time being only, as everything would come to an end if someone from outside our neighbourhood showed up to buy the house.

I scrawled the assistant director's name in my love journal. The notebook had finally found its true owner. Everything was unfolding the way it should. I'll confess that I was doing everything possible to draw the assistant director to me. I was up to my elbows in all manner of superstition and pseudoscience. I put a finger on either side of my temples, constantly trying to send him telepathic messages. I didn't want to go to the boonies to look for him. I didn't want to appear clingy. Being clingy was what an ugly girl would do, but I still didn't want to act like that.

One evening, I was walking along the river when I saw someone fishing. The pole grew taut and arced. It looked like he had a big one. The fisherman had to wind the reel for a while. My mood lightened. Here was a guy, fishing in the middle of the city. Wasn't this river just for people to come toss some floats in the water, for fun? I knew the Chairman would be waiting for me in front of the gates when I got home. I generously congratulated the fisherman. 'You'll have a great dinner tonight!' But then he unhooked the fish and tossed it back in the river.

All the cherry blossoms had fallen. A bounty of green leaves. Flowers and leaves couldn't sprout in the same spot at the same time. It was the end of April, time for midterms at Onjo Junior High. For a split second I lived the life of a popular girl, getting a taste of Dalmi's life. After our math test, everyone rushed over to check their answers against mine. I was confused but gamely showed them my answers. Because I didn't want them to leave. 'Wasn't the first one the right answer?' 'Oh god, I bombed.' 'Wait, I thought it was number one, too.' Everyone was confused. My score ended up being 7 per cent. The rules of probability dictated that I would have gotten 20 per cent even if I'd picked the same answer for every question, but I had scored 7 per cent after solving everything. I should always solve all the problems instead of guessing, I thought to myself. I got similar scores in the other subjects, too.

'Is something going on at home?' asked my homeroom teacher.

'Yes.' Good thing there was. 'My parents were guarantors for someone they shouldn't have trusted. Now our house is up for auction.'

The student disciplinary committee tended to get active after midterms. April, the month of cruelty. May, the queen of the seasons. The weather was nice, the midterms were over, so kids often got lax and started bending the rules. I had nothing to worry about. My name tag was where it should be, I wore my necktie properly and I didn't wear my gym pants under my skirt. My uniform was a baggy sack, bought through the school and untailored. I was walking through the front gates when the dean of students, standing next to the disciplinary committee members, waved his pool cue at me to come over. I looked behind me. There was nobody else. I looked back at the dean of students. He jabbed the air with his cue. *Yeah, you.*

The dean of students reached toward me. I stood still. I even met his eyes squarely. The training I'd received from the assistant director was steeped into my bones by this point, even though it had just been a single day of orders. I was impressed with myself. Maybe the assistant director would reward me if I told him this story. Actually no, he would punish me. Because punishment was the prize during sex with him.

'Did you dye it?' The dean of students fingered my hair. 'You know you're not allowed to dye your hair.'

'I didn't.'

'Then what's this?' He held a strand of my hair up in the sunlight. If he was in this kind of mood, no answer in the entire world would meet his satisfaction.

'It's naturally brown.'

I sensed he wanted to hit me. But he seemed to be suppressing that urge, aware of the other students. Did my face invite beatings? Did the assistant director hit me because I was so ugly, not because it excited him? The dean of students managed to hold on to his dignity. 'Dye it black by tomorrow.'

'I thought we're not allowed to dye our hair,' I retorted and then dashed off to the annexe.

My sister came home often now. Because of the family emergency. She said that there was a buyer despite the blue-eyebrow brigade's efforts. Our idiot parents finally understood the gravity of the situation. My sister transformed from an insane person into Joan of Arc. She sat our parents down to discuss options. Sometimes she showed up before her workday was over. How was she able to neglect her job? Did they let her off because of the situation at home? Or had the person watching everyone left? Had the assistant director gone back to headquarters?

I sent my love journal to him by registered mail. It felt

incredibly meticulous and clever. The addressee had to be the one to accept the registered mail. It would be returned if they couldn't personally accept it. Which meant I was basically tracking the assistant director's location. But what if that turned him off? What a stupid thing to do. I waited for my love journal to be returned. I hoped he was done with whatever he had been doing in the boonies and had returned to headquarters. I monitored the mailbox every day, heart pounding. But my love journal never came back.

I must be more suited to submission than rebellion. The assistant director and I were a match made in heaven. I bought hair dye at the pharmacy. I would dye it super black, a perfectly black colour. A creepy black. Blue-black was popular but I was sick of blue. I draped a sheet of newspaper around my shoulders in Dalmi's living room. Dalmi slathered the dye on my hair. We watched TV while we dyed my hair. She kept accidentally smudging dye on my face.

'I have a question,' I said, moving aside as the brush came too close to my forehead.

'Yeah?'

I needed to take a deep breath in before asking. 'Do you think I'm ugly?'

I'd always wondered what she thought. How absurd it was to ask her this now. I hadn't asked her until then because I dreaded her saying not *yeah* or *no* but *I haven't thought about it*. I was afraid of her indifference.

Dalmi looked at me for a moment before turning back to the TV. We were watching a sitcom. The artificial laugh track went *hahahaha*. The fact that Dalmi looked at me before answering meant she hadn't ever given a thought as to whether I was pretty or ugly.

'Dunno,' Dalmi said, swinging the brush. 'I remember being envious of you because of your pale skin.'

I couldn't help but ask when that was. She said it was when we were little. So when we were in elementary school? I was about to bring up Sein but decided not to.

'But I'm Hongikingan.'

Dalmi didn't bother responding.

In my head, I added, *But now I'm Chichirim.*

The nickname the assistant director gave me. I hadn't told anyone about it. I was dying to brag about it. But I had to keep it under wraps no matter how much I wanted to tell everyone. The more precious something was, the more you had to keep it hidden. The woods where the chichibird lives – Chichirim. Hey, Chichi, so did you find the chichibird?

The aroma of steamed egg wafted over from the kitchen. An aroma that triggered an automatic reflex. Dalmi and I went to the table, babies searching for our mother's milk. My newspaper cape rustled. We were only halfway done. As always, Dalmi finished her food in one minute and went back to the living room to watch TV. I ate with her mum, wearing my newspaper cape, hair dye smudged all around my face. I was glad her mum was the quiet type. I was glad she didn't ask any questions. That day I didn't think I could talk and eat at the same time. The dye reeked. Dalmi must have gotten some under my nose. I felt sick. Dalmi's mum was an incredible cook. Maybe the smell of the dye was making the steamed egg taste fishy.

Everything that happened next was because of springtime. Because the weather was nice. Because the other kids didn't put their name tags on correctly and tailored their uniforms to be really tight and hung out doing karaoke and playing video games instead of studying. Because that made the dean of students take a closer look at everyone. Because the dean didn't know what a natural brown looked like. Because I had to dye my hair to follow the school rules of not dying your hair. I sprinted to the bathroom to throw up. My vomit fizzed light yellow in the toilet bowl. It was so pretty.

9

The flyers weren't what got me hauled into the police station.

I hadn't pasted flyers for the gambling business. I wasn't personally linked to the owner of the gambling business or his wife. And anyway, people didn't go to a gambling establishment because they saw an ad. An ad for a gambling den would actually backfire. That couple had gotten my parents to vouch for them, then they had fled. They had never actually been interested in running a gambling business; it was just something they'd set up to bond with my parents. They had set up their business for the sole purpose of pushing their debts on to someone else and declaring bankruptcy. They had conned my parents, forcing our precious, dilapidated house – Mum's place of work, the blue-eyebrow brigade's living room – to land on the auction block. They had never employed me. They weren't the ones who'd hired me to paste a flyer for ten won a sheet.

I had gone straight home after school. I couldn't go to the hideout anymore. What would I do while Dalmi watched her boyfriend sleep? Would I take up a set of pink blankets and lie there, too, looking up at the ceiling, feeling lonesome? I could sink into my memories but I didn't deserve something that nice. I had broken up with Jinhyeok in the video room. He shouldn't have known what my underwear looked like. He shouldn't have known about my bad habit.

In the main building, they now knew me as the slut. Apparently even a loser with no friends could be a slut. *There's a slut in the annexe! Let's go look.* I didn't think Jinhyeok had approached me to try something with me. To 'tap me', to put it crassly. He wouldn't have done ten almost-flips if that was all he'd wanted. He had risked concussion. Solely to satisfy my mean-spirited requirements. Jinhyeok's feelings for me had been sincere. He had gone out with the ugly girl. He was practically Mother Theresa. We had gone out just so we could break up. Like the pair of swindlers who had opened up a gambling operation just so they could claim bankruptcy, ruining our family.

When I got home, I'd found a police cruiser instead of the Chairman. I had been preparing for this very moment. What I had been imagining every single night was actually happening, in real life. I felt unburdened, finally. I would be sentenced to life for sexually harassing Oksu. After all, I was the one who'd stripped her clothes off. It wasn't Dalmi's hands who did it, nor the hands of her acolytes. Those girls had done nothing wrong. So I opened the back door of the cruiser. I didn't get in the passenger seat. A criminal had to sit in the back, right? The car was empty. I sat there patiently, waiting to be taken in. Had we missed each other? They should have called before showing up. In the cruiser, the door didn't open from the inside. You could enter but not leave. So I had to just keep waiting, since I couldn't leave to go find the cops. It did seem weird for the criminal to search for the cops. It was meant to be the other way around. I sat in the back seat, waiting patiently for my penitent future.

Our front gates opened and my sister saw two detectives off. They got in the front and turned on the radio. They made meaningless conversation, wondering what they should eat for dinner and talking shit about their boss and musing about the weather.

'Hello,' I said.

'Jesus, what the fuck,' they both said, turning in unison to look at me.

The women-and-youth division looked like a kindergarten. The detectives I'd met in their car brought me over to that chilling but adorable space. Two fluffy white clouds held up a rainbow bridge on either end, and the phrase *All of our children represent our shared future* arced over the rainbow, one word per coloured piece of paper. It was a total of eight words, so in addition to red, orange, yellow, green, blue, indigo and violet, they had added brown. It bothered me. My eyes were drawn to the brown. It wasn't a natural brown. I remembered that song, about the dad looking around for his kid on the rainbow hill.

A young female cop poured me some orange juice in a paper cup. I felt sick. I liked orange juice but it felt wrong in this current situation. Just a few minutes ago I had peed into an identical paper cup and handed it to her. Were these cups designed for urine tests rather than serving drinks? I pretended to take a sip and placed the cup on the table. The cop told me smilingly to help myself to any of the snacks laid in front of me. I must have been staring intently at them, counting the remaining coins in my pocket. I was running out of money. I devoured the snacks. I was ravenous. I worried that she would think my parents didn't feed me, which made me wolf them down even faster. My parents were good people. Though they loved each other a little too much. At

least my parents were people. The assistant director was a
monster. Poor guy. I missed him.

'Did the assistant director touch you?' asked the cop.

I spat the cracker, which had become paste in my mouth,
into the paper cup. I thought I needed to say something. I
wanted to ask, *What?* I could have just swallowed it, but I was
feeling the pressure to answer quickly so I ended up being
rude in front of a stranger. Clearly God had made a mistake
when he'd tasked a single organ with two jobs. Though I did
like holding the assistant director's thing in my mouth while
saying *I'm sorry*.

'What?'

According to the cop, I had been brought in because of
Dalmi's mother. The day after I got ill from the reek of the
hair dye and heaved yellow vomit into their toilet bowl,
Dalmi's taciturn mum called Onjo Junior High with a 'feeling'.
A woman's feeling, a mother's feeling, a gut feeling. My
homeroom teacher called Mum. Who didn't pick up because
she was in the middle of a session. The business kept chugging
along even in the chaos of potentially losing our house. She
had to make ends meet. Dad answered his phone but hung up,
believing it to be a prank call. He didn't realize that I went to
Onjo Junior High. I was honoured whenever he remembered
I was his child. My homeroom teacher was green, and still
held an overly strong sense of duty. She asked around and
called my sister in the boonies. It turned out that my sister
was the one who had me arrested! How did she find out what
had happened with the assistant director? Did she snoop in
my love journal? In our dusty room? I was outraged, betrayed.
I was in pain. Pain and bliss could not easily be differentiated.
The way scalding water could actually feel cold.

'Makttungi Uncle is the one who touched me.'

I don't know why that tumbled out of my mouth. My voice had gained a life of its own and burst out of me. Was it my attempt to save the assistant director? No, I wasn't even thinking about him anymore. He had merely brought me, chauffeured in his Chairman, to this moment. He had escorted me to this cop.

The cop inserted a new tape into the voice recorder. She pressed the red button. 'Who's Makttungi Uncle?'

'My mum's youngest brother. She practically raised him. She changed his diapers and he changed mine. He was also born in April. So he came over to celebrate our birthdays together. He was in high school. He was fat because he was a rising wrestling star. So that's why I thought his name was Makttungi Uncle. It was during the IMF financial crisis, so I was six. I was wearing polka-dot panties because it was from the clothing store lady's husband who ran a Ssangbangwool factory that went under. Makttungi Uncle touched me at night, while I was sleeping. He was sleeping on the floor of my room, which I shared with my sister. Our house is old so the living room isn't heated. The storage room was filled with underwear. But it wasn't a storage room from the beginning. It was a regular bedroom. But because we had so much underwear, we had to make it storage. I woke up because my stomach was hurting. He was touching me inside my underwear. I always slept on the outside edge of the bed and my sister slept against the wall. He could only get me when he reached over. My sister wasn't asleep, though. She grinds her teeth when she sleeps but I didn't hear it then. I got up and he pretended to be asleep. I went to my parents' room and tried the door. It was locked. I was tugging on it but it didn't open. They'd never locked their door before. We had accidentally seen them making love a bunch of times. But that day, it was locked.'

Words spilled out of me like I had them memorized. Like I had read and memorized and practised saying them. Of course I hadn't. Years later, at Grandma's funeral, I asked Mum, 'Do you remember the day Makttungi Uncle came over?' Because I had realized that Makttungi Uncle also had a mum. When Grandma was placed into the coffin, he sobbed, saying, 'But my mum hates tight spaces.' I was shocked. Makttungi Uncle has a mum! Well, had. Of course I had known Grandma was his mum, but it still felt strange. 'Why did you lock your door that night?' I asked Mum. She wiped the floor with the towel she had been using to dab her tears. She looked unperturbed. 'I don't remember, maybe it was because he was over.'

At my sister's wedding, I asked Dad another version of that same question. I had asked because my sister had looked so happy on her wedding day. Because Seobin was already in her belly, under her wedding dress. I wondered if she was getting married because of Seobin. At the reception I gave Dad a hard time. 'Dad, why did you lock the front door that time? When I was twelve. Why did you feast on grilled beef without me? You really didn't want to give me any of it?' Dad cried jaggedly, like he had the hiccups. Mum quickly fastened the buckle on her handbag that held the divorce papers, thinking he was crying out of worry that she was going to divorce him.

Ew. That was all Sein had said. We were in elementary school. We'd had fun at the playground. Feeling elated, I'd decided to open the keepsake box inside my heart. I told her about Makttungi Uncle. Back then I thought friendship meant sharing bad things. *Ew.* I hadn't expected that reaction; it caught me off guard. I'd ended up making up ridiculous things. That I had seduced him. That I'd liked how he was touching me. None of that was entirely a lie. Because sometimes that was what I thought. I thought he touched me because I wanted him to. I thought that even after I realized what he had done to me. At the time he touched me, I hadn't known what he had done. After everyone ostracized me, I became obsessed with the idea that polka dots drew guys' hands like magnets. So I sat on top of the lockers in junior high, showing my underwear, in an attempt to prove that hypothesis. I became known as a slut. I liked that. That was a good enough reason.

'She's so patient,' the clothing store lady had said once. A compliment she had cast around for because she couldn't bring herself to utter a white lie. I was not only patient but also had a talent for drawing. My Home Ec. teacher recognized that. 'It's because you look pretty,' said the assistant director at Kimbap Paradise. Telling me that my friends had ostracized me not because I didn't have money for tteokbokki but because I looked pretty. That my friends had been jealous of me. Chichirim, my pretty little Chichirim. The assistant director had a way of simplifying a complicated problem. That reassured me. Makttungi Uncle had touched me because I was pretty.

'Did he insert it?' the cop asked, drawing a geometric shape in her notebook. The kind of thing people doodled when they were on the phone for a long time. 'This Makttungi Uncle of yours, did he insert his penis?'

'He inserted his finger.' If it hadn't been for the assistant director, I would have been too mortified to say words like these. Until recently I had thought I would die on the spot if I uttered any word remotely related to sex. But on our way back to my red-tagged house after that memorable round of sex on Good Friday, the assistant director had made me say obscenities like *cock* and *pussy*. Thank you, kind sir. 'Makttungi Uncle inserted a finger into my vagina.'

I absently picked up my paper cup for a sip of orange juice. The mushy cracker lump was at the bottom. I remembered the pretty yellow vomit in Dalmi's toilet. I wasn't prettier than it.

The cop looked disappointed that only a finger had been inserted, not a penis. She looked disheartened. I almost said, *I'm sorry.* I felt bad that she was disappointed. That Good Sex Friday, I had opened my legs before the assistant director and put my middle finger into my vagina. I had masturbated while imagining my finger to be his penis. I had thought he would kill me if I refused. It hadn't only been awful. Turns out your body reacts even during sex with a murderer. If I had imagined my finger to be his penis, did that mean it was a finger or a penis? Was my finger his penis? Was Makttungi Uncle's finger his penis? A human body was sheathed in just one piece of skin.

'Are you okay?' the cop stood and turned on the humidifier. 'You must be itching because it's spring.'

I stared at the disgusting and beautiful substance in my paper cup. The oil from the cracker swirled on the surface of the juice. It took on a rainbow hue.

'What do you want to be when you grow up?' the cop asked, sitting below the words *All of our children represent our shared future*. The brown construction paper was still bothering me.

'A crab,' I said. 'I want to be a crab in my next life.'

The cop asked about the assistant director. I had to ask, 'Why?' 'Because it's wrong,' the cop said. I confessed and told her all about our relationship. I wanted to see him even if it had to be under these circumstances. I didn't know why our love was being treated like a crime, but I figured I would see him when he came to the station to be questioned. If I couldn't be in his apartment, I wanted to at least see him in this stupid room decorated with clouds and a rainbow bridge. We were going to be set free anyway. All we had done was love each other.

In March, I had gone to the boonies with miyeok guk for my sister's birthday. I had seen the Chairman driving past the cafeteria and heard about the assistant director. He had spotted me from inside his car and realized that I was the bookkeeper's little sister, whom he'd heard so much about. On my birthday, on Wednesday 9 April, I had gone back to bring my sister her spring clothes. She'd given me ten thousand won for my efforts or maybe as pocket money. He had waited for me at the bus stop and I had gotten in his car.

'Wait,' the cop said. 'Who gave you the ten thousand won?'

'My sister.'

Afterwards I had gotten in his car. The cop asked if the assistant director had ever given me money. Why did she care about that? He had never given me money. Did that mean he didn't love me? Mum never gave me an allowance, either. She had made me get a job the moment I entered junior high.

Mum didn't love me. She didn't love my sister, either. My sister had to go to a vocational high school because of Mum. She had to work in the boonies as a senior in high school instead of studying for college entrance exams.

'Why did you get in the car? Did he tell you to get in?'

'No.'

It was hard to explain. He had just been waiting for me in his car. That had been evident. I had gotten in before he told me to get in. We knew each other but we hadn't met yet. We were able to meet because we were able to recall our future.

'Did he know it was your birthday?'

I said yes, which led me down a hellscape of questions. Did you tell him it was your birthday? No. Then how did he know it was your birthday? I'm not sure. How did you know that he knew it was your birthday? Why was she obsessed with my birthday? I was starting to feel important. 'He looked at the cherry blossoms and said I was born on a nice day.'

He had driven me home but we hadn't wanted to go our separate ways. So I had gone to his apartment and played StarCraft with Dongo. The assistant director had grilled beef. He had brought me back home without touching a hair on my head. That was the day his ex-wife came to pick up their son. On Friday 18 April, we'd shared tteokbokki at Kimbap Paradise. And then we had gone to his apartment for Good Sex Friday.

'Did you say you didn't want to? Did you tell him firmly, no, stop? Did you yell that you didn't want to?' She kept peppering me with the same questions she had asked when I'd told her about Makttungi Uncle. But I hadn't said no; I hadn't said I didn't want to. Because I hadn't known if I liked it or didn't like it or what was even happening. I'd just gotten up from bed and gone to my parents' room. To their locked door. Then I'd gone back to bed and lain back down on the edge of our bed. My sister had ground her teeth and Makttungi Uncle had snored. I had smelled cool water.

'No.' I had only been allowed to say *I'm sorry*. I hadn't been allowed any questions. I'd had to do what he wanted so that I wouldn't join the display of corpses. Though of course I had known nothing would stop him from killing me. 'I didn't not want to do it. I wanted to. I liked it.'

I told her all about our Good Sex Friday. She turned off the voice recorder and brought in another investigator. He listened to my story then brought someone else in. I had to go into more detail, then even more detail. *Dongo wasn't at the apartment*. . .I had to remember and remember again.

Nobody doodled in their notebooks.

10

At trial, my sister insisted that my birthday was really in May. She said 9 April was my lunar birthday. She had already read her witness statement out loud. According to what she said, the whole truth and nothing but the truth, I had been twelve years old on Good Sex Friday. A juvenile.

The judge asked Mum about my birth date. Mum said she couldn't really remember. There was no record of it, either. My sister was born in the hospital but I was born at home, in a red rubber basin. Back then, celebrities' births were often featured on TV. The culture at the time venerated water births, claiming it was the best way to give birth. As someone who took pictures of the red tags on all our furniture, gloating that she'd seen it on TV, Mum of course had wanted a water birth, like all the celebrities. But she ended up having me not in a nice tub but in a rubber basin used to make huge batches of kimchi for the winter.

It goes without saying that Dad too didn't know when I was born. Or whether they had registered my birth date following the Gregorian calendar or the lunar calendar. My sister flipped out. 'Dad, even your citizen ID number has your lunar birthday. Of course you used her lunar birthday! Remember, you said you did your military service during your senior year of high school. You said you went back to high school after you were discharged.' The judge warned my sister to settle down. Hesitantly, Dad ventured that he thought he had registered my lunar birthday. He didn't sound confident at all. My sister wasn't all that credible either in the eyes of the law; she was only five when I was born.

'But the cherry tree in our yard had green leaves on it,' she insisted. It was true that she wasn't 100 per cent certain that it was May, but she knew for a fact that it wasn't 9 April. 'I remember because my mum had my sister in the front yard. A green leaf was floating in the basin. It wasn't a pink petal. I was going to scoop it out but the midwife pushed me away.'

'You were born on a nice day,' the assistant director had said as we drove through the pink tunnel. If my sister was right, I wasn't born on a nice day. I was born after all the cherry blossoms had fallen. That had to be why I was ugly. Had the assistant director waited for me to turn thirteen? Because he was afraid of going to jail? Was that why we'd met in April, not March? Because I had gone to see my sister in March, too. I had brought miyeok guk but my sister hadn't eaten it. The Chairman had driven past the cafeteria.

Maybe in the olden days the cherry blossoms bloomed and faded later in the year. Just as girls used to get their first periods when they were older, when the assistant director was a boy. On Good Sex Friday he asked if I'd gotten my period. He had meant whether I menstruated, but I had misunderstood that to mean whether I had my period right then. I'd told him no. We'd made love without protection. A few weeks later I had thrown up my steamed egg. Dalmi's mum had called our homeroom teacher. My homeroom teacher had called my sister. The assistant director and I were reunited in the courtroom.

The case quickly moved on from the question of when I had been born and whether my birth date was by the Gregorian or the lunar calendar. They had already discussed the precise timing of cherry blossom season and global warming. Whether our cherry tree had flowers or leaves on it, whether it had been pink or green, wasn't actually important. What mattered were the numbers printed on official documents. And 9 April was the date I'd become a citizen of the Republic of Korea.

It was a stroke of luck that my birthday this year had fallen on a Wednesday. It was a stroke of luck that Wednesday was the day Dongo was to go back to his mum. It was a stroke of luck that the assistant director happened to have beef in the fridge. It was a stroke of luck that the assistant director had grilled it for me. His attorney argued that the case at hand wasn't about rape but about prostitution. The assistant director had provided me with an expensive meal, a payment of sorts. I was depicted not as a junior high school student but rather as someone already in the workforce. The assistant director had pulled over to answer an urgent call when I suddenly jumped in his car and demanded food. Not that I directly asked for food, but who could look the other way when a dust-covered girl settled in his car, her stomach growling as she sucked on her phone charms? My face burned but I didn't protest. The most important thing was to save the assistant director. His attorney continued that the grilled beef had been payment for sex. Sure, I had eaten it on Wednesday, and we'd had sex the following Friday. But sometimes payments were made beforehand. Mum often took payment before she tattooed her clients' eyebrows. Prepay – that was what it was called.

The trial was like sex. You couldn't ask questions. I had a lot of questions but I had to keep them all to myself. Did he really give me grilled beef just to have sex with me? He had said a pretty-looking girl had to eat something delicious. He had said that was the way the world worked. I could already hear the rumours, *There's a whore in the annexe!* I could see myself being an outcast again. But, for him, I could endure that kind of minimal humiliation. Of course, I didn't think it was prostitution *or* rape. But nobody was interested in what I thought. On appeal, his attorney changed his argument. He claimed that no payment exchanged hands, proving that we were in love. The assistant director had fed me beef but he hadn't given me money. Apparently that was proof of love.

Did that mean Mum loved me?

Time ticked on steadily as the trial continued. At school I took quizzes, played dodgeball, went on a field trip to Everland, took supplementary classes, did my homework, did daily stretches with my classmates, took finals, gave people Mon Chers, laughed, talked, got in trouble, and laughed and talked again. The dean of students didn't make a big thing out of my half-dyed hair. I stayed home all summer break. I didn't go to Dalmi's or the hideout. I took midterms. I took finals. I scored 82 per cent and made my homeroom teacher happy. That would have disappointed her before, but the previous 7 per cent I'd received on my math test helped me out. My sister dragged me to the hospital. I didn't want to go. She manhandled me really roughly, pushed me into the exam room even though I put up a good fight. 'Get in! Get in! You think I'd kill you?' I ended up walking in with my own two feet. They gave me a shot to run some test, but when I opened my eyes I found myself lying on a gurney, wearing a diaper. It felt similar to when I had passed out. Life had gone on for a while, for free. My life had continued on without me. I felt satisfied. *You think I'd kill you?* She was right, she didn't kill me.

Some mistakes can become a blessing. Years later, I had no idea how to react when my sister became pregnant with Seobin. *Why?* was the first question that popped into my head. *A baby? Why? You? Why?* Instead of descending into a hellscape of questions, I just said, 'That's cute.' My sister laughed reflexively. Her laugh was. . .cute. Unfortunately, by then, tact, instead of hatred, had settled between us. She couldn't come to Grandma's funeral because she was pregnant. She didn't have to witness Makttungi Uncle weeping when Grandma was placed into the coffin. *Why did you pretend to be asleep that night? Why did you stick to the wall, pretending? Were you sleeping? Then why were you sleeping? You weren't? Then why weren't you?* I felt just as unmoored when she got married. When she became pregnant with Pancake, my feelings grew even more complicated than when she was pregnant with Seobin. But I quickly felt carefree. Pancake wasn't a mistake. My sister had won this awful game we had been playing for nearly twenty years, though I hadn't even realized we were playing a game. Only after she won did I realize we had been playing this game all along. Good Game.

I can't believe I'm telling you all of this. I hope you don't misunderstand. This isn't a letter of apology. It's definitely not a love letter or a love journal, either. Is it too romantic to call it a farewell letter? Truth be told, I didn't love you. Not ever, not once. Every day, I think about the fact that I don't love you. I think about it every day, every hour, every minute, every second. My not-beloved Chichi, so did you find the chichibird?

At the initial trial the assistant director was sentenced to two years and six months. *As the nature of the crime is heinous. . .*The same verdict was affirmed on appeal. I felt powerless. I didn't deserve to love him. Why should *he* go to prison instead of *me*?

He appealed again.

I wrote a petition on a sheet of A4 paper. It was during social studies and the teacher was drawing a map of the Korean peninsula on the chalkboard, making it look like lightning. He tended not to write on the board very often because he didn't want to reveal the stress-induced hair loss that centred on the back of his head. This was a rare opportunity. I quickly lifted my atlas and wrote on the pure white paper I had hidden below it. I had borrowed the paper from the teachers' office and the pen was a Hi-Tec I had borrowed from Dalmi.

Your honour, if love is a crime, I would be on death row. . .

I couldn't tell if my sincerity was fully conveyed, so I put a sparkly heart sticker on every o. I had bought them at the stationery store when I was gathering supplies for the love journal. With a huge investment of five thousand won, I had bought a sticker sheet, forty-eight coloured pencils and a sparkly pen. The stickers dwindled in proportion to my love for the assistant director. I decorated the petition in rainbow colours. But they never mentioned my petition during the final judgment.

During the third and final trial, Mum and Dad and my sister sat in the witness stand – how dare they. Three owlish judges looked down at us. The prosecutor and the defence attorney battled to define our love. We had to prove our love in court. They would determine if our love was true. When the defence showed the evidence on the big screen at the front of the room, the audience burst into laughter, then cleared their throats in an attempt to maintain dignity. The women sitting in the gallery had the same thick blue eyebrows, eyebrows that made the judges flinch when they entered the courtroom. It must have been pretty freaky for them. The evidence displayed was a page from the love journal I had sent the assistant director via registered mail. A picture of two kissing fish, their lips pressed together, filled the screen. *Kissing fish don't survive the death of their mate. They die from loneliness or from starvation. Oh no! I've become a kissing fish! Because I can't live without you.*

I was proud. My love journal would save him. It would pardon his so-called crime. Which he didn't even commit! If love was a crime, we would be on death row. We would grow old in prison, together, wearing matching red name tags. We would die at the same time, on the same day.

At the time I didn't know that I wasn't the one who'd saved him. My sister had saved him. I didn't know that someone had made a successful bid for our house. The deed was now in my sister's name. She had bid on our house with the forty million won the assistant director had given her as a settlement. Later, that house would be sold to fund the purchase of my sister's marital apartment in Wirye. My love journal, this exculpatory romantic evidence, had not been revealed during the first and second trials for this reason: it had actually been returned to sender. By the time I mailed it, the assistant director had already gone back to headquarters. I had hurled pretty yellow vomit, and my sister had reported the assistant director. He had been sentenced to prison twice. And then they had come to a settlement. Because our house was at risk of being sold to a stranger. My sister had taken the settlement, then dragged me to the hospital. And only then did she hand over my love journal to his attorney. I've already mentioned that she was the one who'd saved him. But she had also been the one who had put him in the crosshairs of the law. Maybe she had put him in danger just so she could save him. All of this manoeuvring was done by the adults. My sister probably knew that I had made the love journal before I even met the assistant director. But she had kept silent about it. Well, whatever. Everything had turned out fine in the end.

The assistant director gave a final statement. He talked about how contrite he was, that he would reflect on how he had brought about social turmoil and stirred up trouble, and if the court could grace him with tolerance and understanding, as the father of a child, he would devote himself to his family and contribute to the growth of the nation. . .Here, *a child* meant Dongo. I started to feel upset. But, then again, I could see myself as Dongo's stepmum. Only later did I find out, by overhearing the neighbours gossiping, that he wasn't divorced. He had only briefly lived apart from his wife while dispatched to the boonies. A separation of sorts, like the situation my parents were in today. Back then, I hadn't known anything. All I cared about was being loved. I was a lovebug, just like Dad. I took after Dad so much that my boobs were smaller than an A cup. In fact, the assistant director had never told me he was divorced. I had made that up on my own.

The assistant director finished his obsequious statement. Instead of directing his question to the defence attorney, the presiding judge asked the assistant director directly if he loved me. I received a public confession of love in court.

According to the final judgment, our relationship had been a product of love. That decision hinged on the fact that my 'love letter' was in colour, not black and white. The presiding judge must not have known what a love journal was. Who would make an entire love journal in black ink? He declared that I wouldn't have decorated it with so many colours and sparkly flourishes if it hadn't been love. That was the logic of the five-minute-long ruling that the judge read out loud. I was happy, but I felt my love fading minute by minute. 'Though we cannot say that the crime is trivial, because the defendant does not have a prior criminal record and has reached a settlement with the individual acting in loco parentis for the plaintiff, and the plaintiff does not wish for the defendant to be sentenced. . .I declare that the defendant is acquitted.'

With three back-to-back trials, that year sped by. I entered the eighth grade. The kids who had been in the annexe in seventh grade were all assigned to classrooms in the main building. A portion of the new seventh graders who had been randomly assigned to Onjo filled the three classrooms in the annexe. Their bad luck. I was fascinated that there were kids younger than me at school now. I was fascinated that kids were being born every year. Of course there was a weird kid in the seventh-grade class. He wanted to do rock-paper-scissors with everyone he saw. He did rock-paper-scissors, then, after he won or lost or tied, challenged someone else to a round of rock-paper-scissors. I thought of Dongo. I couldn't tell if I missed him or not. Dalmi and I weren't in the same classroom anymore. I became best friends with her acolyte. Our friendship was based on our shared experience of stripping Oksu naked in the auditorium the previous year. I kept bumping into Jinhyeok in the hallways or by the water cooler. We avoided each other.

I joined the art club. I went to various lame drawing contests and lamely placed third. I asked my parents to send me to private art classes. Not because I was really all that passionate about art; I just wanted to ruin myself and our family as well. Mum took to bed, deeply upset. Dad made a huge deal of it, bringing her water and checking her temperature. Their furious opposition and their grieving expressions flamed my love for art. My sister said she would support me. She was living back home, having been fired in retaliation for her role in the prosecution of the assistant director. My parents had no say in anything now that she owned our house.

I hated them all.

After some time, my parents started talking divorce. There wasn't a specific incident that caused their rift. Maybe because late-in-life divorce was becoming more popular. Honestly I don't know exactly why. I'm sure nobody knows. One day, Mum left, and for a while it was just Dad and me. And then it was time for me to go to college, and I left. My sister was working in another part of the country as the bookkeeper at a small company. She married a reliable, stable guy. A deputy section chief at the same company. She sold our house for a hundred million won to buy their new apartment. Before the sale, I went back and burned all the remaining polka-dot panties in the yard. Otherwise my sister might have saved them for Seobin. I didn't love Seobin but didn't want her to wear that tainted underwear. The branches of the cherry tree were bare. My parents pushed off divorce again.

Inertia overtook me after I burned the piles of underwear. I threw out or sold everything I owned. I closed bank accounts and deleted apps off my phone and erased the phone numbers of people I hadn't contacted recently. I settled my affairs. I threw out my shampoo and bodywash and switched to an all-in-one product that smelled like cool water. I ended up with pruritus. I drunk-dialled my ex and told him I wanted to eat his mum's soy-marinated raw crab. Then I deleted his number. I did freelance work and frequented dermatologists. I paid my sister back for the money she loaned me. I gave Seobin a packet of Haribo. The neighbourhood doctor told me not to suffer through the itchiness. I made Chiruchiru's clothes a solid colour, got rid of the rainbow in the night sky and turned everyone's eyebrows back to a normal colour. I drank Jerusalem artichoke tea.

Twenty-seven days after Seobin's nine hundred days of life, Pancake was born. My sister's in-laws were anxious in case they had to return the blue baby clothes they had prepared. Only after they heard the words 'a beautiful baby boy' did they relax. He had ten whole fingers and toes. While my sister was recovering in the hospital room, our parents, her husband, his parents and I were shown to where Pancake was. I stood there, my forehead against the glass pane. Oh, right, Makttungi Uncle was there, too. He stopped by on his way home after judging a wrestling match at Jangchung Gymnasium to celebrate the birth of his great-nephew. He had started working as a referee after his restaurant closed. He came to the hospital with a bouquet of flowers. I wasn't sure if he'd bought them or stolen the bouquet meant for the winner of the wrestling match. Not that it mattered. What mattered was that it was a bouquet. It was just a bouquet no matter who held it. Was I feeling at peace because Pancake wasn't Seobin? Because Pancake was a beautiful baby boy? Not that any of that mattered, either.

On the other side of the glass, a nurse picked up a baby among countless identical newborns. The way someone working at a fish market picked out a fat halibut and hoisted it up with a net. Everyone exclaimed. Dad took advantage of this touching moment to put an arm around Mum's shoulders. Who shrugged him off.

'Are you getting a divorce?' I whispered to her. They had no more excuses now that Pancake was born.

My voice must have carried because I felt Dad tense up beside me. Dad did whatever Mum said. He would do anything, even if it was signing the papers. And then he would kill himself. Thankfully Mum didn't answer me. She was agog over Pancake. Dazed. Did she wear the same expression when I was born? In the red rubber basin in the yard?

The nurse brought Pancake close to the glass so we could see him better. Like she was forcing us to find him adorable. My brother-in-law was on the verge of tears. His parents clapped. Dad looked at Mum, and Mum looked at Pancake, both with a smile. Makttungi Uncle rustled the bouquet. I stared straight at Pancake and wondered what I was supposed to feel. That nearly pushed away the fact that I don't love you. Chichi, my dearly un-loved Chichi, you aren't Pancake. Pancake isn't you. How weird. You aren't there, among all those babies.

Mum slid a hand in her purse and fingered the divorce papers. I slid my hand in my pocket and fingered the envelope of cash. Earlier, in the waiting room, my brother-in-law had handed me the envelope. 'Sorry,' he'd said, 'but I overheard your parents talking. I heard you borrowed tuition from your sister. Use this to pay her back. Don't tell her I gave it to you.' I tried to give it back, telling him I'd already paid her back, but he told me to keep it, that I could buy the kids treats when they were older. Why did I have to take on this burden? He didn't know that their home in Wirye was purchased thanks to the settlement my sister got in return for my extreme sexual acts. She was only eighteen at the time. I took the envelope of cash. I didn't care about money so I would probably just give it to my sister. She was the one who was obsessed with money, not me. *Your husband gave me pocket money*, I would say. *You take it. Don't tell him I gave it to you. And don't give it to Mum and Dad, either.*

'Hey.' My brother-in-law elbowed me, his forehead pasted against the glass. His breath formed a circle of fog on the pane, disappearing before fogging it up again. 'How does it feel?'

'How does what feel?'

'How does it feel to be an aunt?'

He must have entirely forgotten about Seobin's existence.

Which was the same for me, too. All babies were the first to ever be born.

'Hm.' I stepped away from the glass. 'Cute.'

There was a Kimbap Paradise in front of the Supreme Court. Which made sense but was shocking all the same. We were waiting for the final judgment. The court was in recess. Even a trial had to pause for meals. Our family of four sat around a table for the first time in a long while. We studied the menu. Mum and my sister ordered tonkatsu and I chose tteokbokki. Kimbap Paradise was where I, Hongikingan, had been reborn as Chichirim. The woods where the chichibird lives. I couldn't help but feel nostalgic.

We set the table and poured water into cups while Dad agonized over the menu. He couldn't choose between the options. *Why don't you just lock the door and grill some beef all by yourself*, I thought snidely. Mum pointed in exasperation at the wall behind us. 'Just eat that.' I turned to look. At the poster on the wall.

KKONGchi KIMchi JOrim.

Braised mackerel and kimchi.

The first syllables were enlarged for emphasis. My eyes were naturally drawn to the second syllables of each word. I choked, started coughing. Who knew I could cough and laugh at the same time? I laughed and coughed, laughed and coughed. I even got the hiccups. I might have thrown up if my stomach hadn't been empty. But nothing remained in me. The woods shuddered, rustled. But then everything calmed. As though Chiruchiru and Michiru had gone home after their adventures.

'What's wrong with you?' My sister thumped me on the

back, irritated. Mum pulled the paper-thin napkins from the dispenser and handed them over. Dad raised a hand to order. My nose stung and tears clung to my lashes. But I didn't cry. I was happy. My name is Chichirim. KkongCHI kimCHI joRIM – Chichirim.

That day, I was still the plaintiff, and, in the future that I could remember, the defendant hadn't yet been acquitted.

Author's Note

Thank you, Minumsa, for publishing *The Woods Where the Chichibird Lives* in South Korea. Thanks to my Korean editor, Kim Jihyun, who polished my sentences like they were her own. Thanks also to Minumsa executive director Michelle Nam and Kim Dajeong in the foreign rights department; they were instrumental in bringing this novel to the English-language world.

My gratitude to Romilly Morgan at Brazen – thank you also for coming up with the wonderful English title *The Crustacean*. Thanks to Chi-Young Kim, who eagerly took on the translation of my book. I am indebted to her meticulous and exact counsel, and I wish her all the happiness.

I'm grateful to the Seoul Foundation for Arts and Culture, the Arts Council Korea, and the Sojeon Foundation for supporting my work. Thank you to the creative writing department at my alma mater, Seoul Institute of the Arts. I'd also like to thank my supportive family and friends.

My sympathies and consolation to the three billion people worldwide who are living with itchy skin. As I suffered from symptoms that came out of nowhere, I believed this one thing – since they appeared out of nowhere, couldn't they disappear out of nowhere, too? And in fact, one day I was suddenly healed. So many things happen like that. I very much hope for a world where nobody is itchy.

Finally, from the bottom of my heart, I thank you, the reader, for buying and reading my novel.

About the Author

Jang Jinyeong began her literary career in 2019 by winning the New Writer Award from Jaeum and Mo-eum. She has published several short story collections as well as two novels, including *The Crustacean*, her first to be translated into English. To date, *The Crustacean* has sold around 17,000 copies in Korea.

About the Translator

Chi-Young Kim has translated more than 20 books. She was awarded the Man Asian Literary Prize for her work on *Please Look After Mom* by Kyung-sook Shin, and her translation of Cheon Myeong-kwan's *Whale* was shortlisted for the 2023 International Booker Prize.

This brazen book was created by

Publisher: Romilly Morgan
Acting Publisher: Ella Gordon
Creative Director: Mel Four
Senior Developmental Editor: Pauline Bache
Editorial Assistant: Emily Campbell
Copyeditor: Ian Critchley
Typesetter: Six Red Marbles
Production Controller: Sarah Parry
Sales: Lucy Helliwell and Natasha Photiou
Publicity & Marketing: Charlotte Sanders and Ailie Springall